Alive and Dead

Martha Crayle worked for an association for unmarried mothers and thought she knew all their problems. But the blonde girl who strayed into her office one wet November afternoon posed a new one, for Amanda was pregnant but she was not unmarried. Therein lay the germ of a situation which was to involve Martha in a new and frightening world of crime.

Amanda's husband had been dead three years, or so everyone but Amanda insisted. But how could the same man be alive *and* dead? And what about the body recently discovered in the hotel opposite Martha's office? Were the police right in believing it was Amanda's husband and that she was a murderess? Or were others who knew Amanda right when they claimed quite sincerely that the girl was out of her mind? Only Martha seemed determined to befriend her, and Martha's devoted friend, Mr Syme. And Martha was soon in grave danger, for the truth behind Amanda's astonishing assertions was more bizarre than anyone could have guessed, and was to lead Martha to make a number of unexpected discoveries, not least discoveries about herself.

Alive and Dead

Elizabeth Ferrars

THE THRILLER BOOK CLUB
LONDON : 1975

The Thriller Book Club,
125 Charing Cross Road,
London WC2H 0EB

First published in Great Britain 1974

This edition by arrangement with
William Collins Sons & Co. Ltd.

Printed in Great Britain by
Biddles Ltd, Guildford, Surrey

The National Guild for the Welfare of Unmarried Mothers is an entirely imaginary body and has no connection with any body in existence devoted to the same work.

E.F.

CHAPTER I

IT WAS just before five o'clock that the gentle knock came at the door.

Martha Crayle had been about to leave the office. She had put on her overcoat and was looking at herself in the mirror over the fireplace, knotting her scarf over her head. The coat was scarlet and the scarf was of green and scarlet checks. She liked bright colours. She was a shortish, sturdily built woman of fifty-three who was often taken for less because her movements still had the energy of someone much younger, her short, toughly curling brown hair had no grey in it, and the expression of her round, widely spaced blue eyes was one of innocent youthfulness. Nothing that had ever happened to Martha, and a good deal had happened to her in her time, had ever deprived her of that look of hopeful candour.

She was glad to hear the knock, even if it meant that she could not leave for home just yet. She had had the office entirely to herself all the afternoon. Olive Mason, the Secretary, was down with flu and Lady Furnas, the Chairman, was away on a cruise in the Caribbean. And not a single caller had dropped in. So Martha had had no one to talk to and had been distinctly bored.

She had had her knitting with her, part of a knitted dress that she was making for herself, but she was not really a dedicated knitter. As an accompaniment to cheerful conversation she was not against it, though the results of what she did somehow seldom quite satisfied her. But simply to knit on and on by herself in a drab, empty office, which was not as warm as it might have been, was not what she thought of as a rewarding way of spending her time.

She would have been better off if she had brought her

transistor with her, but Olive Mason had never suggested that she should do that and Martha was not sure how it would be regarded if she did. This business of being a voluntary worker could sometimes be tricky, and she was anxious not to displease anybody. It was important to her, working conscientiously and regularly as she did, to think that she was a help, was valued.

The knock at the door was softly repeated.

Arrested in front of the mirror, her head-scarf knotted under her chin, Martha called out, 'Come in!'

The door was opened with diffident caution.

There was no need for the caution. The lettering on the door, under the notice that said 'National Guild for the Welfare of Unmarried Mothers' said, 'Enquiries.' The caller had every right to walk straight in and do her enquiring.

But just as her knock had been shy, her way of entering showed that she wanted to be as inconspicuous as possible. She slipped in, closed the door noiselessly behind her and stood still just inside it, breathing quickly.

She looked about twenty-four. To Martha, who had been developing an eye for such things since she had come to work here as receptionist, the girl also looked about three months gone. Her normally slender body had only just begun to thicken. She was wearing a dark blue and green tweed coat on which raindrops glistened, dark slacks and muddy, flat-heeled shoes. Her long, light golden hair was flattened damply to her head and there was a sheen of moisture on her face, which was oval and very pale, with delicate features and noticeably large grey eyes that looked nervously at Martha out of deep hollows of exhaustion. The girl was carrying a small suitcase which Martha, who was observant about certain things, noticed was of good leather.

She did some quick summing-up. A girl from a well-to-do family who gave her expensive presents, like the suitcase, but who had turned her out because of her condition, or perhaps from whom she was hiding, afraid to let them discover it. Not that you saw much of that sort of thing nowadays. Most families seemed resigned to accepting the illegitimate offspring of their young as part of their own responsibilities. But occasionally you encountered the patterns of the past.

'Well, come in,' Martha said. 'You look awfully wet. Come and sit down by the fire.'

The fire was only a small electric heater that shone with a dim red glow in the empty Victorian fireplace. The Guild did not waste any of its scanty funds on comforts for its employees.

The girl did not move.

'You're closing,' she said. 'I'm too late.'

An educated voice, low-pitched, pleasant, hopeless.

Martha undid her head-scarf and dropped it on the desk.

'I was only getting ready to go because nothing was happening,' she said. 'I'm in no hurry. Come and get warm.'

She sat down at her desk, switching on the lamp at her elbow, which showed up the shabbiness of the small room, the dull green walls that had not been painted for a decade, the battered desk, the hard, unwelcoming chairs. There was nothing to brighten the place up but a vase of chrysanthemums on the desk, which Martha herself had brought that day from her own garden, and a calendar on the wall, sent for some mysterious reason the Christmas before by a local garage, and showing a picture of the main street of the town flooded from end to end with a rainbow river of cars.

'It's a horrible afternoon,' she said. 'How long have you been trailing around in the rain?'

'Ever since . . . I came down on the bus from London this morning because I thought I could . . . I mean, I didn't think of the difficulties, so I just started . . . I don't know how long exactly . . .'

The girl seemed incapable of finishing a sentence. She still did not move from just inside the door.

'So you've been hunting for a room all day, have you?' Martha said.

The girl nodded.

'And they took one look at you and said they were full up.'

The girl nodded again.

'So you thought of trying us.'

'Yes, but . . .' The girl pushed back a wet strand of hair from her face. 'I'm not sure if you can help me.'

'Nor am I,' Martha said. 'I know the Helsington Hostel's full. Anyway, they wouldn't take you in without all sorts of checking up. But come and sit down and just tell me a few things about yourself.' She took a form out of a drawer and picked up a ballpoint pen. 'Please don't look so scared. If we can help you, we will.'

'Yes, but . . .' The girl seemed about to stick at that point, then went on in a sudden rush. 'On the door it says you help unmarried mothers.'

'Yes, that's right,' Martha agreed.

'But I'm married, you see.'

Martha laid the pen down on the desk and sat back in her chair.

'That does complicate things a bit, I suppose,' she said.

'Probably it means you won't help me now,' the girl said.

'Well, technically speaking . . .'

Martha paused. Normally this was the point at which she would have gone and consulted Olive Mason, who, in any case, was the person who would have had to make some decision about the case. Martha's job was only to get a few particulars from the applicant for help and keep her comfortably chatting until Olive was ready to see her. But with Olive ill and Althea Furnas in the Caribbean, Martha had to think for herself.

'Technically speaking,' she said, 'the office is closed and I'm only a voluntary worker. I've no authority and I don't know if I can do anything for you anyway. But if you'll come and sit down I'll make a cup of tea and we can talk about your problem.'

The ghost of a smile passed briefly across the girl's pale face.

'You're very kind. When I came here I thought a social worker would be – well, difficult. But that was silly. I don't know why one thinks such things. One shouldn't take people for granted. Any more than they should take one for granted oneself. They shouldn't think they know what's best for one without finding out what one really feels. Do you think they should?'

Martha went into the little scullery that opened out of the office. She filled the kettle and plugged it in. Putting teabags into the teapot, she called back over her shoulder, 'Are you really married?'

Often the girls who came here said at first that they were, though they had a way of wanting to tell the truth about themselves in the end.

'Oh yes,' the girl said. There was a pause. 'But it isn't as simple as that exactly.'

'I didn't think it would be.'

There was no irony in Martha's tone. She was hardly ever guilty of irony. It was just that in her own experience nothing to do with marriage had ever been simple. Her two husbands had left her for reasons that she had never understood. She had believed that they were happy with her, and then suddenly each of them had up and gone. The first one had said that she was intolerably domineering. The second had said that she was such a doormat that it brought out all the worst in him and that he could not bear that. It had been very puzzling. And each of them had left her with a child who had had to be cared for and educated. Well educated. From the first Martha had had ambitions for her children, although neither husband had ever paid her the maintenance to which the courts had said that she was entitled. She might have fought for it, of course, but that would have been a sour, unpleasant thing to undertake. It had come more naturally to her to shrug off the past, get herself work and manage alone.

That had been before Aunt Gabrielle had come into her
life and made everything easy. So easy that now, with the
boys both grown up and doing well in their different ways,
Martha could treat herself to the luxury of taking a job for
which she was not paid. A job of some sort was a necessity
to her. That was one thing that the long, difficult years had
done to her. She would have found it intolerable to stay
idly at home all day.

Bringing the tea-tray into the office, she found that the
girl had at last sat down near to the small electric heater.
Martha poured out a cup of tea for her, then one for herself.

'I'm sorry, we seem to have run out of biscuits,' she said.
'That's because our secretary's been away the last few days
with flu. It's the sort of thing she always remembers.'

'I'm not at all hungry,' the girl said. 'But the tea's nice.
Thank you.'

'If you're married,' Martha said, 'what's really your problem? Have you left your husband?'

The girl gave a very slight shake of her head. She was
looking down pensively into her teacup and it seemed for a
moment as if she did not intend to make any further reply.
Martha, watching her, thought that if she had looked
happy, if there had been any light or animation in her
face, she would probably have been beautiful. But the only
expression in the big grey eyes was fear.

That seemed very sad to Martha. She had had to fight
most of her own fears by herself, without much assistance
from anyone, but she found that fear in another person
called up all the protectiveness in her nature.

'What is it then?' she asked. 'Or don't you want to talk
about it?'

The girl went on looking into her teacup.

'He left me,' she said. 'Three years ago.'

'Oh, I see,' Martha said. 'You mean the child isn't his.'

'No.'

'And what about the child's father?'

'He's a student. A PhD student. His subject's Social Science.'

'I meant, does he know about the child?'

'Oh yes, I've been living with him until just lately.'

'Does he want the child?'

'I – I think so. He was upset at first, but now he says he wants it.'

'Then just exactly what's the difficulty? Couldn't you and your husband get together somehow and arrange a divorce, so that you and this other man could marry?'

The girl raised her head and gave Martha a long, odd stare.

'Perhaps,' she said, 'only I'm not sure if I want to marry Don. He's got some – queer ideas about me.'

'You've left him, have you?'

'Yes.'

'How long ago?'

'A week. I've been living with my family since then. But I can't stay with them. That's quite impossible.'

'Why?'

Martha's relations with her own family had always been cool but pleasant. Her father had been a freelance journalist, feckless, gentle, much wrapped up in himself and the dire problem of making a living. Her mother had been a shy, thoughtful woman, difficult to know. But in times of crisis they had never abandoned Martha.

The girl's fine eyebrows twitched nervously together.

'Because they're trying to make me have the child adopted,' she said. 'They want me to have what they call a new start in life, pretending none of it ever happened. And that's the one thing I don't want to do. What I want is to think things out for myself. That's why I came away.'

'What made you choose Helsington to come to?'

For Helsington was not a place to which many people

bothered to come unless they had good reasons. It was a small, rather characterless town in the south Midlands, with some light industry on its outskirts and some pleasant country round it, but nothing in the town itself to attract to it, in the middle of November, a lonely, desperate young woman who wanted the right sort of surroundings in which to do some serious thinking. Martha herself had come there from London many years ago because of the offer of a job, and gradually, without quite knowing why, had settled in so that now she only very occasionally thought of leaving.

'I just happened to remember it,' the girl said. 'My grandmother used to live here and when I was a child we often used to come here to stay with her for the summer holidays. She died years ago and I haven't been here since, but I remembered it as a place where I'd been very happy. And I thought all I'd have to do was to go to a boarding-house and ask for a room to stay in for a bit. After all, this isn't the holiday season. I didn't think the place would be crowded. But perhaps because I brought so little luggage with me, and then got wet and looked rather miserable, and with my being pregnant too, everyone turned out to be full up. So I came here to see if you could tell me what to do.'

'How did you hear about us?' Martha asked.

'By accident, really. There's that hotel opposite and I was standing in your doorway downstairs to get out of the rain, and wondering if I should give up the idea of looking for a boarding house and see if I'd have better luck with a hotel, though I couldn't afford one for more than a night or two, when I saw that notice of yours by the door, saying you were here on the second floor. And it seemed quite extra-ordinary and much too good to be true, but I thought I'd just come up and see . . .' She paused. She had put her feet close to the fire and her wet shoes were beginning to steam. 'I don't really want to go to a hostel or anything like that,' she said. 'But I thought perhaps you'd be able to advise me what I ought to do.'

'Why don't you go back to London and your Don?' Martha suggested.

'Oh no!'

'Does he know where you are?'

'He probably thinks I'm at home.'

'But your parents must know you've left. What will they think?'

'They'll think I'm with Don. They won't worry.'

'But suppose they get in touch with him and they find you've vanished, won't that be rather hard on them?'

The girl drew down the corners of her mouth, which gave her face a momentary look of vengefulness, almost of ugliness.

'I don't mind what they think. They shouldn't have tried to make me have the child adopted. I want to have my child. I want to keep it. They shouldn't have interfered.'

'No, I suppose they shouldn't. It doesn't usually do any good. Have some more tea.'

'Thank you.' The girl gave Martha her cup and as Martha refilled it gave a deep sigh. She was beginning to look more relaxed. 'You're wonderfully kind. And I expect I'll find somewhere to stay all right. Don't worry about me.'

'I was just thinking . . .'

As a matter of fact, Martha had really started thinking about the matter some minutes ago, when she had been out in the scullery, making the tea, but she had not wanted to rush things. Rushing things, she knew, was a bad habit of hers. Yet her second thoughts were very seldom different from her first thoughts. Once an idea had entered her head, it generally carried her away.

'You said you just want a chance to think things out, didn't you?' she said.

'Yes.'

'For a few days?'

'That's all.'

'Well, I've actually got plenty of room at home myself,'

Martha said. 'I used to run a boarding-house, but I got left a legacy, so I was able to stop working, and the place is empty, except for Mr Syme. He was one of my oldest boarders, and I hadn't the heart to turn him out. But he wouldn't bother you. He's very good at keeping to himself. So I could easily let you have a room, though you'd have to look after yourself mostly, because I'm out a good deal. But I dare say you wouldn't mind that. You'd at least have a place to rest and have peace and quiet. What do you think about it?'

'What do I *think*?' The girl's face grew suddenly, beautifully radiant. Her eyes in their shadowy sockets shone. 'Do you really mean it? Just like that? You don't know anything about me.'

'Well, you'll remember I'm just making this offer on my own account, won't you, and not on behalf of the Guild? They insist on references, and medical reports, and investigating backgrounds to make sure you're really desperate for help, and so on. But I generally make up my mind very quickly about people, and if you'd like one of my rooms for a few days, you're welcome. But you mustn't expect much. It isn't at all grand.' Martha, uncertain how luxurious the home might be from which the girl had fled, was quick to fear criticism of her shabby old house.

'If you knew how wonderful it seems . . .'

'Then drink up your tea and we'll go.'

Martha felt pleased now that she had made her offer. As she had said, she made up her mind very quickly about people, and though it was only occasionally that she found herself actually disliking anyone, her normal attitude to the human race being one of almost all-embracing tolerance, there were people to whom she took more of a fancy than others.

'Of course, I've sometimes put people up for the Guild officially,' she said, standing up and picking up the tray. 'Sometimes if we've had a particularly sad case and the hostel's full as it is now and yet one's felt one simply had to do something, I've helped out. That house of mine is really so big, you see. I suppose it's stupid of me not to have sold it and got into something smaller, but it's such an effort house-hunting, and it's nice to have somewhere for the boys to come home to – I've two sons, you know, and one of them's just got married and I'm soon going to have a grand-child – and then there's Mr Syme, who'd be horribly un-settled if he had to find somewhere new to live. So some-how I've never thought seriously of moving.'

She had taken the tray into the scullery and was speaking over her shoulder again as she rinsed the cups under the tap and tipped the teabags into the bin under the sink.

There was silence in the room behind her. All of a sudden Martha had a feeling that the room was empty, that the girl had gone. She turned back to the door.

The girl had not gone, but she had risen to her feet, crossed to the window and was standing there, looking out into the rain.

She was standing singularly still and there was an intent-ness in the way that she was gazing out into the dusk that made her look as if she were watching and waiting for something important to happen.

But there was nothing much to be seen from the window but the windows, on the other side of the street, of the Compton Hotel, a high, flat-faced, concrete building, with a flashy portico, outlined in neon, and row on row of iden-tical windows, some of which were lit up already, while others were still dark, with empty rooms behind them. There was a good deal of rush-hour traffic in the street and the pavements were crowded with people hurrying along under bobbing umbrellas. That was all.

Dismissing the puzzle of the girl's attitude as probably no more than a symptom of the state of tension that she was in, Martha took her own umbrella from the peg on the wall where she had hung it when she arrived, and tied her scarf over her hair again.

'Let's be going then,' she said.

On their way downstairs one or two other people who were leaving offices that opened on to the narrow, shabby staircase called out good evening and made remarks about the shocking weather. She chatted with them as she went down, followed by the silent girl, whose face, Martha noticed as the two of them reached the doorway at the bottom of the stairs and stood there nerving themselves to step out into the driving rain, had become as pinched and pale again as when she had first come into the office.

Opening her umbrella and holding it so that the girl should get some protection from it, Martha took her arm and they started off up the street. It was a narrow street, a turning out of the High Street, with most of its houses, except the Compton, built of dingy red brick, meant once as good, middle-class residences, but which with time had mostly slithered downhill into shops and offices. Perhaps because the street led to the Infirmary, a great many of the shops were medical supply shops, with their windows filled with strangely shaped objects of steel and plastic, which in daylight could promise gleaming and efficient help to the suffering human body, yet which in the dark could become eerily threatening, even mocking the weakness of flesh and bone, compared with their own lifeless strength. As always, at this hour, the traffic was dense. The rain hissed on to the wet paving stones and gurgled in the gutters. A gusty wind threatened to snatch the umbrella from Martha's grasp.

'It isn't far,' she said. 'Are you all right? Can you manage it? Perhaps I ought to have rung up for a taxi, only you can never get them in weather like this, just when you want them.'

'No, I'm all right,' the girl said. 'I'm fine.'

'It's got so cold today. You're really all right, are you?'

'Yes, I'm fine.'

They struggled on in silence towards the corner of the street.

Suddenly the girl exclaimed, as if the thought had only just occurred to her, 'Do you realize you don't even know my name?'

CHAPTER II

'MARTHA, you must be certifiably insane,' Mr Syme said. 'To bring a girl home like this when you hadn't even asked her name.'

'Well, it was she who thought of that and wanted to tell me what it was,' Martha answered. 'Not that I see that a person's name is so very important. The question is, does one like them?'

'You like everybody,' Mr Syme said, as if he did not find this one of Martha's more admirable qualities. 'And Amanda Hassall is only what she *says* her name is. I can't say it sounds particularly authentic to me.'

'Why ever not? And anyway, does it matter?'

'Giving a false name is an indication of untrustworthiness.'

'But you've no reason for thinking it's a false name.'

'Except that I'm afraid I find myself instinctively distrusting the young woman.'

'You distrust everybody,' Martha said, giving him back the blow that he had just given her.

He frowned coldly. He was looking his iciest, most forbidding self, as he had looked ever since Martha had arrived home with Amanda Hassall and he too had just arrived home after his day in the library and they had all met in the hall of the echoing, empty Victorian house in Blaydon Avenue, a wide curving street lined with fine old chestnut trees, which had once been one of the best streets in Helsington, but now was largely given over to guest-houses, nursing-homes and offices.

Martha could remember the time when most of the square, sober houses had still been inhabited by families with large numbers of children who had played conkers with the chestnuts that they had collected from the gutters, ridden bicycles, with Red Indian war whoops, up and down the street, and played football and cricket across it. But now the place seemed to be given over entirely to the parked cars of the people who came to work in the nearby High Street. It was only at night that Red Indians could have roamed in it again, under the shadows of the great trees, in the sudden silence that descended when all the cars had been driven away.

Mr Syme had not been discourteous to Amanda Hassall. He was never discourteous. But he had failed to join in the mirth which had been engendered in the kitchen, after two gins and tonics all round, when the fact that Martha had asked Amanda home to stay without even discovering her name had begun to strike the two of them as wonderfully funny. Amanda's pale cheeks had turned pink and her melancholy had dissolved in giggles. It had cheered Martha just to see it. But Mr Syme had not seen the joke. As Martha and Amanda had grown more and more exuberant, he had grown more and more formal, abrupt and unapproachable.

They had had supper in the kitchen, a supper of soup and bacon and eggs, since the chops that Martha had bought for herself and Mr Syme would not have been enough for three people. Then there had been cheese and coffee and then Martha had sent Amanda off to have a hot bath and go to bed in the room furnished in somewhat battered mahogany, where they had made the bed up before supper and which smelt a little musty from disuse, but was not actually damp. Martha had taken Amanda's clothes away and put them in the airing cupboard to dry overnight, then had returned to the kitchen where Mr Syme lingered because, of course, he wanted to give her a lecture, and she had poured out whisky for them both and settled down to listen to him.

A good many of the long talks that they often had with one another were conducted in the kitchen with a bottle of whisky on the table between them. The kitchen was really the most cheerful room in the house, now that all the boarders except for Mr Syme had gone, and Aunt Gabrielle was dead, and the boys had left home. Martha used it as living-room and dining-room, as well as doing her rather rough and ready cooking in it.

It was big and old-fashioned, with an earthenware sink and old wooden draining-boards instead of a shiny, stainless steel sink-unit, an old black cooking-range, which was never lit, because Martha did her cooking on an almost equally antiquated gas stove, a big deal table that needed scrubbing instead of merely wiping over, as a modern plastic-topped table would have done, and an ancient sofa, covered by a tartan rug to conceal the places where the stuffing was coming through the covering.

But the walls were white, there were primrose yellow curtains, some bright-coloured pots and pans hanging from hooks, a television and a bookcase full of paperbacks. Martha felt much more comfortable there than in the chill propriety of the sitting-room across the hall.

That room housed most of Aunt Gabrielle's more precious furniture and Martha had not yet brought herself to alter anything. Aunt Gabrielle had chosen and furnished most of the house. It was the kind of house in which she had grown up before marrying her Canadian husband and going away for fifty years to Montreal. She had not returned to England until after her first stroke, which had happened five years after her husband's death, and which, in loneliness and illness, had brought her home to seek out her only living relations, Martha and her sons, to see if they could help her.

She had not come begging, however.

The old woman had seen to it that any arrangement that they came to should be of advantage to them all. If Martha would look after her, she had suggested, she would supply a home for her and pay all the weekly bills. To Martha, who at the time had been working as a checker in a supermarket in Helsington, living in a too-small flat that overlooked the noisy bus-depot and wondering how she was going to get the boys the education on which she was determined, the offer had seemed overpowering in its generosity.

She had not thought then of taking in boarders. She had started that only when she had come to realize that Aunt Gabrielle did not understand about the rise in prices. Without her having the faintest intention of being stingy, the money that she had given Martha every Saturday had not been nearly enough to keep the family fed. Martha could, of course, have tried to explain this, but as she had with her two husbands, she had found something repellent about the idea of arguing about money. Anyway, she had liked the thought of not being entirely dependent. Yet she had been very fond of the old woman and when Aunt Gabrielle had had her second stroke and had progressed from merely a slight lameness and absent-mindedness to almost complete paralysis, incontinence and a gentle, doddering senility, Martha had looked after her with devotion and love and an ungrudging sense of obligation.

The boarders had mostly been young people, students at the new university in Helsington, or nurses at the hospital, or school teachers. It had been hard work looking after them, but Martha liked being surrounded by people and had enjoyed it. Only the shock of discovering, when Aunt Gabrielle died, that she had left her, besides the house, a legacy of fifty thousand pounds, had made her decide to empty the house and give herself a rest.

A rest which had lasted for only three months. By the end of that time she had felt in such need of employment that she had taken on the voluntary job of receptionist for the National Guild for the Welfare of Unmarried Mothers, a job into which she had drifted more or less accidentally, through the chance of becoming acquainted in a friend's house with Olive Mason. But once Martha had settled in she felt that the job had almost been made for her. She had

never been technically an unmarried mother herself, but she
had had to face the world alone, with two children to bring
up, and her feeling for the girls who passed through her
hands, who would probably never have any Aunt Gabrielle
to help them and whose future problems she understood
only too well, was intensely sympathetic.

Far too sympathetic, Mr Syme said. Often dangerously
sentimental.

'Insane,' he repeated, over the whisky that Martha had
just poured out. 'You've no idea what trouble some of these
girls might get you into.'

'Darling, you know you only say that because you don't
like meeting strange young women on the way to the bathroom and things like that.'

Martha generally called him 'darling', or 'Edward dear',
because that was the sort of thing that she called most
people, and she did not want to hurt his feelings by seeming
to set him apart. But at the back of her mind she always
thought of him as Mr Syme. It was because of his air of
steely dignity, the impressive modelling of his high forehead
and bald head, the penetration of his cold grey eyes, his
appearance of intellectual distinction. He was sixty-seven,
moderately tall, a little portly. He had been Town Clerk of
Helsington until his retirement, living for most of his life
with an elderly housekeeper, on whose death he had been
as distracted as he might have been at the loss of a wife.
Not knowing how to organize his existence then, he had
drifted into Martha's care for what, it had been clearly
understood, was to be a few weeks. And he had stayed for
ten years. When Martha had given notice to the rest of her
boarders to quit, she had not had the heart to disturb Mr
Syme.

He occupied two rooms on the first floor, into which he
had moved his vast collection of books, and he spent most of
his time in the local library, gathering material for his History of Medieval Helsington, and he appeared, after his

fashion, to have developed a deep affection for Martha, and to believe that without him to look after her interests, her thoughtlessness and what he called her immaturity and her readiness to take everyone at face-value would bring God knew what disasters on her head.

'Not at all. It's you I'm thinking of,' he said, facing her across the kitchen table. 'You know nothing of this girl's background. You know nothing of the young man she's been living with, or these parents who are supposed to want her to have the child adopted. Suppose they're all thoroughly undesirable types. Suppose that young man tracks her down here and suppose he's unbalanced, violent, breaks in here, turns on you, even assaults you. She seems afraid of him herself, doesn't she? Certainly she's afraid of something. And one would imagine that she didn't leave him for no reason at all. Or suppose none of these people exist at all. You've only her word for it that they do. The real truth about her may be something quite different.'

Martha widened her round blue eyes at him.

'The things you think of!' she said. 'Unbalanced. Violent. What things to suggest. As a matter of fact, I know perfectly well what's happened.'

'You mean the girl's told you more than you've told me?'

'No, I've told you everything. But think about what's happened to her. She married young. It must have been young if her husband left her three years ago. Then after a time she started living with this other man, Don Somebody. And probably that was just because she was lonely and didn't get on with her family, and she never meant it to be anything serious. But then finding she was going to have a child and not trusting this young man to look after her and the child as he should, and realizing she'd probably have to carry the load of looking after the child by herself anyway, she just felt she had to get away from him to think things out. So she went home again. And then her awful parents tried to compel her to have the child adopted. That would be the last straw. Of course she had to get away.'

'You've worked all that out because it's the sort of thing that happened to you at her age,' Mr Syme said. 'You've no evidence that her parents are awful. They may be very sensible, kind people who know that the young man is worthless and that the girl herself is irresponsible and neurotic and not fit to bring up a child by herself.'

'But I think it's awful to try to make her have the child adopted if she wants to keep it,' Martha said.

'You've only her word for it that they've done that.'

'Well, why should she say they have if they haven't?'

'God knows. To play on your sympathy, no doubt. But why do people tell half the lies they do? Usually it's for no rational reason whatever.'

'But we don't know this *is* a lie. I'm sure it isn't.'

'Even though she's told you one other obvious lie? Doesn't it make you at all suspicious of her?'

Martha wrinkled her forehead at him, meeting his sharp grey eyes with uncertainty. 'I don't know what you mean.'

'She lied about her reason for coming to Helsington,' Mr Syme said. 'She says it's because she spent happy holidays here with her grandmother. But when I asked her where her grandmother used to live, she went very red and said she couldn't remember the name of the street.'

'I don't see anything odd about that,' Martha said. 'She was only a child when she used to come here.'

'It's just the things that happen to one as a child that one remembers best,' Mr Syme said, 'particularly if one's been as happy as she claims to have been. And I'll tell you another thing I don't believe. I don't believe she was just walking down that street and happened to notice your Unmarried Mothers notice by chance, and came in on the spur of the moment. I think she sought you out. I think she came to the office deliberately, because someone had told her to.'

Martha reached for the whisky bottle and topped up both their glasses. The whisky felt comforting after the long, damp, tiring day, and she always enjoyed her evening chats with Mr Syme, even when he was lecturing her.

'Where's the harm in that?' she asked. 'Isn't it what we're for? All this fuss you're making. None of it worries me in the least. Nearly all our girls lie to us. And Amanda may have all sorts of good reasons for not wanting to tell me why she came to Helsington. That's her business.'

He sighed. 'As I've often told you, you suffer from a pathological trust in the human race. Not that I would have you otherwise. I just wish your trustfulness were tempered by more discretion. One day I can see it getting you into serious trouble. And who knows, that time may just have come.'

'Well, I'll tell you one thing that *is* rather worrying me,' Martha said. 'I really sympathize very warmly with Amanda, and if she wants a place to stay for a little while till she's sorted out her feelings, she's very welcome here. But even if her parents and that young man are terrible, I can't help feeling she ought to let them know where she is. Or at least that she's all right. After all, such frightful things happen nowadays, and if she simply walked out on them without letting them know why, they may be frantic with worry by now. They may be thinking that she's been run over and killed, or that she's drowned herself, or been raped and murdered.'

'I was just about to say something to that effect myself,' Mr Syme said. 'I'm very glad you thought of it yourself. We shan't get embroiled over it in one of our useless arguments.'

'Oh, we never get embroiled,' Martha protested. 'We always agree perfectly in the end. This evening you haven't meant a single thing you've said. You've really agreed with me all along.'

Mr Syme thumped his glass on the table. 'I have not! It's one of the delusions you suffer from, that I always agree with you. I do not!'

'You know in your heart you do.' She usually believed that most people felt as she did and so very seldom wanted to argue with them. It was one of the things in her which her first husband had insisted was a kind of bullying, since she was trying to impose on him far finer emotions than he felt. 'But she really must let her parents know she's all right, mustn't she? Or they might even start the police hunting for her, and wasting their precious time when they ought to be stopping bank-robberies and things like that. Yes, I'll tell her in the morning she's got to telephone her parents and tell them not to worry.'

'Tell her she can't stay here if she won't do that. Tell her you can't take the responsibility of actually hiding her.'

'Yes,' Martha said, nodding. 'I'll definitely do that.'

However, next morning, although she did her best to be definite, she found herself up against a definiteness in Amanda Hassall a good deal greater than her own. The rather ethereal-looking girl had, it appeared, a will of iron.

'No,' she said, 'I'm sorry if it worries you, Mrs Crayle – but no.'

Amanda had appeared for breakfast with her long, fair hair slicked back behind her ears and with her shoes and her dark slacks carefully brushed. She was wearing a brightly patterned tunic which almost hid the early signs of her pregnancy, and she had some colour in her cheeks after what she said had been a wonderful night's rest.

'Really I'm sorry if it worries you,' she went on, 'but I can't face getting in touch with anyone yet. What delicious coffee you make.'

She was sitting at the kitchen table while Martha, still in her dressing-gown, roamed about the room. Mr Syme had had his breakfast a little earlier and had retired to his room rather more hurriedly than he usually did, in order, Martha supposed, to avoid the risk of having to converse with the girl.

'I've been doing a good deal of thinking since I woke up

this morning,' Amanda continued. 'I was too tired to think last night. I just fell into bed and went to sleep. But this morning I've been thinking. I can't tell you how grateful I am to you for taking me in yesterday. It was marvellous of you. I'll never forget it all my life. But of course I can't go on exploiting your kindness. So I'll go out and start looking for somewhere else to stay. It's a nice bright day and I feel quite different from yesterday. I'm sure I'll be able to find something.'

'Honestly, there's no need for you to leave,' Martha said. 'But I don't like the thought of what your parents must be feeling at the moment. Having sons of my own, I know how easy it is to get frantic with worry if they're out only an hour or two longer than they said they were going to be. Of course one has to control oneself or they get resentful, but still I've been through agonies on their account and I really do feel for your parents.'

'Tell me about your sons,' Amanda said, spreading butter and honey on a piece of toast. 'Are they like you?'

'I don't think so,' Martha replied. 'I think each of them is far more like his father. Martin, the older one, is a very solid citizen. He's a chartered accountant, and he's always rather uneasy about me, because he doesn't feel I'm as settled in life as a mother of his ought to be. And Jonathan, the younger one, is unbelievably good-looking, and he's recently married a very rich girl who's keeping him while he hammers away at making rather obscene but really quite beautiful little figures of wrought iron, and he's beginning to make quite a name for himself and I expect he'll end up richer than she is. I'm very proud of them both. And they're both wonderfully good to me. They're not much for writing letters, but they often ring me up, just to have a chat now and then, sometimes at simply enormous expense. Isn't that sweet of them? But . . .' She stopped, realizing that she had been sidetracked. 'It's not my sons we were talking about, it's your parents. I don't say you've got to tell them exactly where you're staying, but I do think you should tell them you're not in the river.'

The honey on Amanda's toast was dripping over the edge of it on to the table as she held it halfway to her mouth and gazed at it abstractedly.

'They'd be glad if I was in the river,' she said.

'I don't believe that – that's a terrible thing to say!' Martha exclaimed. 'Listen, my dear, you've absolutely got to let them know you're all right. About Don – well, I don't know. I wouldn't think of interfering between you and him. But I do know how parents feel, even when they don't show it much, and I do insist that you telephone them and tell them not to worry about you.'

'You don't understand.' Amanda noticed the dripping honey and scraped it up with her knife. 'It isn't that they don't show their feelings. They show them all the time. They smother me with them. And they're always dead sure they know what's best for me. But the one thing they won't ever do is listen to me. They won't let me talk to them. They won't believe I mean what I say. And they're always talking about how much they love me and how I ought to love them in return, as if you can *make* a person love you, whether they want to or not. And the awful thing about it is, perhaps I could love them if only they'd leave me alone. That's all I need just now – to be left alone. And that's why I simply won't telephone them now, you see, because if I spoke to them they'd appeal to my conscience, and they'd say what about having the child adopted – it's that that I can't forgive. And . . .' She paused. Her voice had been rising. After a moment she added quietly, 'No, I won't speak to them. Not just yet.'

'I wish you would.'

'No.'

Martha sighed. 'All right then. But you needn't feel you've got to move out. You can keep your room for the present, if you want it.'

The girl's rare smile, which lit up her pallid face with peculiar radiance, made it glow for an instant.

'Now if only someone like you was my mother, I'm sure there wouldn't be any problem,' she said. 'We could talk to each other about anything. The way your sons telephone you from all over the place, I'm sure that's because you never tell them they ought to and because they truly love you. D'you think they know how lucky they are? But I really don't want to go on exploiting you. I'll go looking for another room this morning. And perhaps I might find a job of some sort too. I feel awfully well. I could easily do a job for the next few months.'

'But I thought you only wanted a quiet place to stay for the next few days,' Martha said. 'This is the first you've said about a job. Are you planning to hide from your parents and Don for weeks or months?'

The girl's eyelids drooped swiftly. She bit into her toast and honey.

'I don't know. It was just a sudden thought.'

Her face had closed. Whatever she felt was hidden behind an odd, nervous expressionlessness. Dismayed and uneasy, Martha took her own plate and cup and saucer to the sink and began to wash them up. Behind her the girl's chair scraped suddenly as she stood up, then walked swiftly out of the kitchen, leaving her cup of coffee half full.

Martha heard her presently leave the house. She had already heard Mr Syme leave for the library. Soon afterwards she went up to the bedroom that the girl had occupied, meaning to strip the bed. It was Martha's regular day for going to the launderette and she meant to include Amanda's sheets in her bundle. But she found that the bed had been left neatly made. Had that been a mere automatic action on the girl's part, Martha wondered, or did it indicate a perhaps unconscious intention on the girl's part to return in spite of the fact that she had taken her small suitcase with her? In any case, the bed could be left as it was.

If she did not return, the sheets could go into next week's wash. Martha left the room and went to collect Mr Syme's sheets and towels, then got dressed in a tartan trouser suit and set out to do the morning's shopping.

It was from two o'clock until five that she worked for the National Guild for the Welfare of Unmarried Mothers. Although Olive Mason worked in the office from nine in the morning until five, it was only during the afternoon that it was open to the callers who were Martha's concern. Not all of them were unmarried mothers by any means. There were the social workers who were associated with the work of the Guild. There was a nice young parson who was sympathetic to its aims but who came to the office mainly, it seemed, because he enjoyed a chat with Martha. There were one or two doctors. There were parents and foster parents and people from the adoption societies.

Today, when Martha arrived punctually at two, she expected, since Olive was ill, that the office would be empty. But while she was still on the landing outside it, she heard voices inside, Olive's and another, which Martha did not recognize. She opened the door and entered.

Olive was sitting at Martha's desk. Martha's first impression of her was that she would have been sensible to stay at home, for her face was pale, her eyelids were red and she was mopping at her puffy nose with a damp tissue. Her greeting when Martha appeared was an attack of coughing.

'Sorry,' she gasped in between one cough and the next and pulling a new tissue out of her bag. 'I hope I don't pass this on to you. But they tell one the infectious time is before it comes out, don't they? Once one really starts hawking and spitting one's harmless. So I thought it'd be all right if I came along today. I get so bloody bored if I stay at home. Besides, I think of all the damned work piling up here and it starts me worrying.'

Olive was much addicted to mild swearing. She was a

solidly built woman of thirty-five, big busted, broad hipped, with straight very fair hair which she pulled straight back from her face and rolled up in a plait at the back of her head. She was very fair-skinned and because of the pallor of her eyebrows and lips, and the fact that she never used any make-up, her face had a curiously naked look. This afternoon she was dressed, as it sometimes seemed to Martha that she always was, in a dark green pullover and cardigan and green tweed skirt, with a necklace of large, artificial pearls.

'Let me introduce Miss Aspinall, a new client,' Olive went on. 'Sandra, this is Mrs Crayle, our receptionist, whom I've just been telling you about.'

A girl who was sitting by the little electric fire where Amanda Hassall had sat the evening before met Martha's eyes with cheerful black ones, surrounded by circles of magenta eye-shadow, and said, 'Hallo.'

'Hallo,' Martha responded.

Sandra Aspinall was about the same age as Amanda Hassall, but that was the only resemblance between them. This girl had a round face with brightly rosy cheeks and plump lips which were touched up with almost lilac lipstick. She had a short, pert nose, a dimpled chin, and thick, dark hair that fell in a tangled mane to her shoulders. She had a small, alert-looking, very neatly shaped body, clothed in a close-fitting black jersey dress, with a bright orange girdle round her waist. If she qualified as an unmarried mother, she so far showed no sign of it.

Olive's fit of coughing subsided.

'Martha, Sandra and I have just been talking about you,' she said. 'I've been telling her about how you've helped us out once or twice before and how just possibly you might be willing to help her now, because she's really got a devil of a problem to sort out. What I personally think a bloody tragic one.'

Sandra grinned and said, 'That's right.'

No one could have looked less tragic than she did. But that could have been simply because she had more courage than most. It was hard to tell.

Martha already knew what she was about to be asked, but said automatically, 'What can I do?'

'It's just a question of whether you could put her up for a few days in that big house of yours,' Olive said. 'The problem is, you see, that the young man who Sandra thought was going to marry her will only go through with it now if she has an abortion, even though he admits he's the father of the child. But she won't hear of anything like that, and I'm on her side, a hundred per cent. You know the Guild doesn't hold with abortions except on real medical grounds. So as soon as that little bastard started talking about that sort of thing, she came to us. She'd heard of us from the curate of the church she goes to. And she just wants us to find her somewhere to stay for a few days while she looks for a room and a job for the next few months. And by then, of course, if we've put her name down, we ought to be able to fit her into the hostel. But for the next few days she does need somewhere to stay, and so – but don't hesitate to say no if it's inconvenient – I thought of you.'

'Oh dear,' Martha said. 'All right – yes.' But to herself she added, 'Oh dear, poor Mr Syme!'

CHAPTER III

THE AFTERNOON was a quiet one. Olive retreated to her office, which opened out of Martha's, and the expert tapping of her typewriter started as she got to work on the letters that had accumulated since she had been ill. Sandra settled down with one of the very out-of-date magazines that the Guild kept in the office for its visitors and Martha got on with her knitting.

She was working on the back of the dress now and she had reached the stage of wondering what had ever made her start, for she had a feeling that it would never be finished. The telephone rang a few times and she put the calls through to Olive, whose voice, as she answered, was very hoarse and was interrupted by spasms of coughing. But when Martha called out a suggestion that Olive should go home to bed, she asked what the point was of going to bed if you had no one to look after you and you had to get up to get your own meals. She really felt better working, she said.

Olive lived in a small flat not far from the office, but normally did not spend much of her time in it. Besides her work for the Guild, she sat on a number of committees in the town, worked hard for the Conservative party, played the viola in a quartette, belonged to a women's luncheon club, and generally was so involved in the activities of Helsington that Martha, who thought of herself as a fairly gregarious person, often wondered where Olive found the time and the energy to fit them all in. Yet Olive often complained with a good deal of bitterness about her loneliness, and it was true, Martha thought, that in a sense Olive seemed to be friendless. She was not hospitable. Martha had known her for three years now but had been into her flat only two or three times, and although they sometimes had lunch together, or drinks in the pub near the office at the end of the day's work, they were really no more intimate than they had been when Martha had first started working for the Guild.

They got on well enough, however. There had never been the slightest friction between them. Yet something stopped Martha this afternoon mentioning to Olive that she had invited Amanda Hassall to her home. Martha knew that Olive liked to feel that she was fully in charge of everything in the office. Even Lady Furnas, Chairman of the local branch of the Guild, usually did quite meekly what Olive told her to do.

Presently an even longer outburst of coughing from the inner office made Sandra Aspinall call out, 'Miss Mason, wouldn't a cup of tea do your throat good? Can't I get you some?'

The girl had been getting restless and wandering here and there about the office. At this moment she was standing by the window with a look of irritability on her plump, rosy face.

'That reminds me,' Martha said, 'we've finished the biscuits. Shall I pop out and get some? There's a little other shopping I want to do too. Would you like me to get you some lozenges, Olive?'

Olive appeared in the doorway of her office.

'There's something you might do for me, if you would,' she said. 'I've got a prescription to pick up at the chemist. I left it with him this morning and said I'd collect it in the lunch hour, but with Sandra turning up I forgot. Would you be an angel and get it for me, Martha? And some lozenges might help, if you know any good ones.' She held out the receipt for the prescription.

Martha took it, put on her coat and started out.

At the bottom of the shabby stairs she found the door to the street blocked by a man who was standing just outside the door, apparently staring intently at the hotel on the

other side of the street. But for an unusual air of intentness
about him, Martha might not have noticed him. People
often lounged in that doorway, sheltering from wind or rain
as they waited for the buses that came to the nearby bus-
stop. But this man was not lounging. When Martha, finding
that she could not edge past him, murmured, 'Excuse me,'
he sprang out of her way almost as swiftly as the hero of a
Western reacts when someone sticks a gun in his back.

Then he caught his breath, muttered, 'Sorry,' and as soon
as Martha was out on the pavement, moved back to where
he had been standing before.

She took away with her an impression of tallness, thin-
ness, touzled red hair and curiously shining, angry eyes.
Then she forgot him as she battled her way against the
strong wind that caught her as soon as she was out in the
street.

Although today was dry it was much colder than it had
been the day before. Massive clouds chased one another
across a wintry sky. The air was full of gritty dust, some
tattered autumn leaves and scraps of flying rubbish. Martha
buttoned her coat up to her neck, wished that she had put on
her head-scarf, and hurried along as fast as she could past
the medical supply shops, with their constant reminders of
how lucky you were to be walking around at all on your
own two feet, to Olive's chemist.

He was round the corner in the High Street, a long,
straight street with all the usual chain-store shops in it, as
well as an old coaching inn, the Crown Hotel, generally
reckoned a much better hotel than the Compton, and a
really fine Elizabethan Town Hall. There was a queue at
the prescription counter in the chemist's and Martha had
to wait for a quarter of an hour before she was able to
obtain Olive's tablets. Then, as there was a Marks & Spen-
cer's next door, Martha went in and bought a chicken for
dinner. She would have four people to feed, and she had
nothing at home but the chops that she and Mr Syme had

not eaten the evening before, and more eggs.

Having bought the chicken, she bought a packet of stuffing, some frozen peas and the biscuits for the office tea. Altogether her shopping excursion took her at least half an hour. So it seemed surprising to her that the same man who had blocked her way when she left the office should still be blocking it when she wanted to re-enter.

He was still staring with his odd, fierce stare at the Compton Hotel. The Compton had never struck Martha as an object of much interest. It was said to be quite comfortable, with a bathroom and television for each of its diminutive rooms, and reasonably good service, yet how anyone could be filled with as much emotion about the place as this man seemed to be was puzzling. If it had been the Crown now, it would have been different. The Crown was all black beams and small casement windows and worn old steps and crooked floors. People were always stopping to stare at and photograph the Crown. But the Compton was even more uninteresting than the terrace of houses that it had replaced three years ago.

On an impulse Martha spoke to the man as he moved out of her way once more.

'Miserable day,' she said.

He did not answer. He was younger than she had thought at first, not more than twenty-five.

'I hate this wind,' she added. 'I almost prefer rain.'

He gave her a lowering look, for a moment transferring his mysterious anger from the Compton to her, then gave his attention back to the hotel.

Martha, going up the stairs, felt rather offended. He might at least have said that the weather was seasonable, or even nice and fresh. Gentle argument about the weather forms an important part of civilized behaviour. It is the ritual by which people can signify their kindly interest in one another.

But perhaps the young man did not want anyone to take

an interest in him. Perhaps he did not like being noticed. Perhaps he was up to no good. Or perhaps he was a detective, watching for someone to come out of the hotel.

That was an intriguing thought. It made Martha smile to herself as she went into the office, gave Olive her tablets and lozenges and started to make the tea.

But Olive did not wait to drink it. Chewing on a lozenge, she said she thought that her temperature was going up again and that after all she ought to go home. She certainly did not look at all well. There were patches of red on her cheekbones, while the rest of her face was very pale.

'I'd go home too, if I were you, Martha,' she said. 'I shouldn't think anything important's likely to come up now. Oh, and I almost forgot to tell you, this postcard came from Althea this morning. She'll be home on Saturday.' She tossed a picture postcard on to Martha's desk. It showed palm trees, blue sea, yellow sand and the faces of one or two grinning black children. 'I'm sure I'll be back before then, but she's certain to come in on Monday anyway. Goodbye for now, Sandra. Anything you're worried about, ask Martha.'

She went out.

When the door had closed behind her, Martha and Sandra sat sipping tea for a little while. Then Sandra said, 'Mrs Crayle – please tell me – is it really all right for me to go home with you?'

Her voice had the classless, nasal whine popularized in recent years by the BBC. Martha could make no guess at her background. She only found it somehow surprising that the girl should have been sent to Olive by a clergyman. Sandra did not strike her as probable church-going material. But with the young you could never tell. You never knew what they might try out next. And you couldn't tell much about present-day clergymen either.

'Just so long as you don't upset Mr Syme,' Martha answered. 'He's a lodger of mine and he likes to be the only

one. He doesn't like it when he has to share my attentions.
He takes it almost as a personal insult. And I took another
girl home yesterday, so he's badly put out already. She
came here yesterday just before I closed the place up, and
of course Miss Mason wasn't here, so I couldn't consult her,
and the poor thing was so wet and so frightened that I didn't
know what to do with her, so I took her home. And Mr
Syme was very annoyed. So he'll probably be even more
annoyed this evening. But if he's a bit grim to meet, don't
worry. He's immensely good-hearted.'

The goodness of Mr Syme's heart was an article of faith
to Martha. It did not require proof. So it did not matter to
her if not many other people had found evidence of it.

'Frightened?' Sandra said. 'What was she frightened
about?'

'Mostly not being able to find anywhere to stay, I suppose,' Martha answered, 'and I think being afraid she might
have to go back to her family, who seem to have been
putting a lot of pressure on her to have the child adopted.'

'Oh, I see,' Sandra said. 'I know that kind. They send
you away for a nice holiday abroad, which is really a trip
to a nursing-home, and when you come out everything's
been taken care of and there's no scandal and everything's
lovely, and you can get married later and have some more
babies and you just never have to worry about what happened to the first one. For all you know, it's been brought
up as the child of an earl. Anyway, you can always tell yourself it has.'

'Have you any family, Sandra?' Martha asked.

Sandra shrugged her shoulders. 'Yes, and they're all right,
I suppose. But my Mum and Dad never got on and when
I started having boy-friends my dad used to say "like mother
like child", and seemed quite glad to get rid of me. So I
didn't hang around.'

'Where do your parents live?' Martha asked.

'Out at Hemlow.'

Hemlow had once been a village about ten miles out of Helsington, but developers were rapidly turning it into a suburb of the town, with a straggle of bungalows joining the two together.

'My father's a farmer,' Sandra went on. 'People always said to me how lucky I was to grow up on a farm, with lovely fields all round to play in, and lovely fresh eggs to eat from lovely hens, and milk from lovely cows. But I'll tell you something funny, Mrs Crayle, I've always been terrified of cows. I know they aren't going to hurt me, but I'm dead scared to go near them. I'm just naturally a town girl. But listen, are you really sure it's all right about me coming to your house? I mean, with you having this other girl staying with you, and your Mr Syme being difficult, I wouldn't want to be any trouble to you. The way Miss Mason asked you to give me a room, I could see you could hardly refuse, but I could easily go out and get a room somewhere else. Honestly, I'd much sooner do that than be a bother.'

'No, that's all right. By the way, where's your boy-friend and what does he do?' Martha asked.

'He's a printer. He works in London.'

'Does he know you've come to us here?'

'Not yet. But I thought I might phone him to tell him where I was. I mean, I've got nothing against him, even if I've left him, and I don't want him working himself up about what's happened to me.'

'Nothing much against him and nothing much for him either,' Martha observed. To keep her own relationships on just such a level was what she had striven for for the last twenty years, though not often with success. People were always becoming more important to her than she intended. 'Is that how it is?'

'Yes, that's just about it,' Sandra said, 'though I've never thought of putting it like that. But mind, I'd like to go overboard about someone sooner or later. I mean, I'll never know what I'm missing till I do. But it won't be with Derek.'

'Well, I suppose we might as well be going home, since Miss Mason said we could,' Martha said. 'I don't think anything more is going to happen here this evening.'

A few minutes later they started downstairs, Martha carrying her shopping-bag and Sandra her suitcase. The wind was blowing as hard as ever and it was even colder than it had been earlier in the afternoon. Martha paused in the street doorway to tighten the knot of her head-scarf. Her gloved hands fumbled with the knot and as they did so she happened to glance across the street.

The red-haired young man whom she had seen standing in this doorway an hour or so ago had just come out of the Compton Hotel. But now he was not alone. Amanda Hassall was with him.

Amanda was in her blue and green tweed coat, with her fair hair spread out over her shoulders. She was carrying her little suitcase. Something seemed to be the matter with her. She was sagging against the man as if she could hardly stand and even from the other side of the street Martha could see that the girl's face was blank with shock. He took a grip on her elbow and began to hurry her along, walking with long strides, so fast that she stumbled, trying to keep up with him. Martha saw the man give her a shake, saw the girl try to wrench her arm away and the man's grip obviously tighten.

Martha's immediate impulse was to run after them. If this was the father of Amanda's child, if he had somehow managed to trace her and meeting him had the effect on her that it seemed to have had, then someone ought to go to her help. But just as Martha was about to dash across the street through the momentarily stationary traffic, the traffic-lights at the corner turned green and the traffic surged forward. Before there was any gap in it Amanda and the man had disappeared round the corner.

'What's the trouble?' Sandra asked, looking at Martha curiously as she teetered at the edge of the pavement. 'Is something wrong?'

'I don't know. I hope not. Perhaps not.'

But even if there was nothing as seriously wrong as Martha feared, what had Amanda been doing in the Compton Hotel? Could she have been looking for a room there? Had she felt it was so wrong of her to impose on Martha's hospitality that she could not stay on for even a day or two more? Yet she had said yesterday that she was not sure that she could afford to go to a hotel for more than a night or two.

Then there was the problem of how the man had known that she would come there. In spite of what she had said about him, had she had an appointment to meet him in the Compton, and had perhaps her lateness in keeping the appointment been the cause of the anger seething inside him that Martha had sensed when she had seen him first?

'You do look worried,' Sandra said as they started along the street towards the corner into the High Street. 'Something's upset you, hasn't it?'

'No, just puzzled me,' Martha answered. 'It's nothing much. I expect it'll sort itself out presently.'

But perhaps, she thought, the chicken in her shopping bag would have to feed five people. For if Amanda should make peace with the young man and bring him home, one could hardly refuse him a meal. So perhaps it would be wise to pop into a shop and buy some ice-cream to help out the tin of peaches that she had intended to open. And some more bread might be necessary. Turning these matters over in her mind, Martha forgot the sharp uneasiness that she had felt on seeing Amanda and the red-haired man come out of the hotel together.

In Blaydon Avenue the pavements were thick with tawny leaves, wrenched from the tall chestnuts by the day's fierce wind. They squelched underfoot and at times were treacherously slimy. The parked cars that by day formed ramparts along the edges of the pavements, were beginning to depart. Martha pushed open her gate. It had a distinctive squeak which announced the arrival of anyone at the house before the bell had been rung or a key pushed into the lock. While she still had her key in her hand the front door opened. The squeak had summoned Mr Syme. So almost certainly, Martha thought, Amanda had brought the man home with her, and Mr Syme, deeply shocked and put out, had been lurking in the hall, listening for Martha to tell her what he thought of her for letting this kind of thing happen.

She was taken aback when she saw that he did not look deeply shocked and put out, but blandly welcoming. It was true that when he saw Martha his expression altered. It became one of slight irritation and he said, 'Oh, it's you.' So apparently he had been expecting someone else, perhaps one of his friends whom he had invited in for a drink. He occasionally entertained friends in his rooms, though usually he preferred to meet them at his club or in one of the local pubs. His rooms were a very private place, where even the cleaning woman, employed by Martha twice a week, was only grudgingly allowed to enter. But at least his equanimity must mean, Martha thought, that Amanda had not brought the unknown man home with her.

Martha was wrong. As soon as she stepped into the hall, a place only dimly lit, even in day-time, because of the stained glass panels in the window, and which had a steep staircase with iron banisters rising up from it, and a floor of tiles in a depressing pattern of cream and brown, she heard voices coming from the sitting-room.

'You've got to, don't you understand?' a man's voice said. 'Do as I say. You've no choice.'

'Oh, Don – please!' The voice was Amanda's. Martha recognized it although it was thick with tears. 'Just give me a little time. I've got to have time to think.'

'But there *is* no time,' the man answered. 'Christ, Amanda, for once you've got to face the truth!'

'The truth!' she cried. 'Who hasn't been facing the truth till now?'

Martha advanced to the doorway. Mr Syme caught at her sleeve.

'Martha, will you have the goodness to tell me who this young lady is?' he demanded.

He and Sandra were looking warily at one another.

Martha paused. 'Oh, I'm so sorry, I'd forgotten I hadn't introduced you. This is Miss Aspinall. She's coming to stay with us for a few days. Sandra, this is Mr Syme.'

'Not – ' There was a slight tremble in Mr Syme's voice. 'Not *another*?'

'Well, yes, as a matter of fact,' Martha said. 'Olive asked me to look after her. And don't say we know nothing about her, because she was sent to us by the curate at Hemlow, so that should set your mind at rest. And she won't get in your way at all – will you, Sandra? – so you've nothing to worry about. Now just wait a moment, Sandra, then I'll show you your room.'

She went on into the sitting-room.

It was a big room with a high, heavily moulded ceiling. Aunt Gabrielle had been very proud of it. It had white and gold wallpaper, a Chinese carpet, a number of velvet-covered chairs and sofas and some water colours, executed by a friend of Aunt Gabrielle's, mostly of Canadian pine forests and lakes and waterfalls in the mountains.

Amanda was sitting on one of the sofas. She was still in her blue and green tweed coat. Her suitcase was on the floor beside her. Her fair hair, which was wind-blown, hung wispily about her face. It was blotchy from crying and her cheeks were wet. The red-haired young man was standing over her with both hands on her shoulders, as if he had just been shaking her.

He straightened up when he saw Martha. He was about six foot three, wide-shouldered but gaunt, and was dressed in a black leather jacket and the jeans that are the uniform of his generation. Amanda, blowing her nose, came to her feet at his side.

'This is Don,' she said. 'Don Turner. Don, this is Mrs Crayle.'

He was looking at Martha with an uncertain air of recognition. But he seemed to have forgotten where he had seen her before and to dismiss it as unimportant. He looked as if he found her altogether unimportant. She was just a bothersome intrusion into something that really mattered. His shiny, angry eyes had a glare of arrogance in them. But he was better-looking than Martha had realized in her earlier glimpse of him. He had a high, square forehead, a short, straight nose with a broad bridge to it, a narrow-lipped but sensitive-looking mouth and a firm, bony jaw. And in spite of the chronic anger which seemed to be the only expression to which his face was accustomed, it was an intelligent one, or so it seemed to Martha, and because she had a deep respect for intelligence, believing that people who possessed it in any outstanding degree were in a different category of human being from herself, she found herself more inclined to take a favourable view of him than she had been prepared for.

'I don't know how you found Amanda,' she said. 'I suppose she must have changed her mind and telephoned you after all. I'm glad. I was rather worrying about how you'd be feeling if you knew about her disappearing. But I won't have you intimidating her. Not while she's here. I suppose you're staying at the Compton.'

He gave a slight start and said, 'At the *Compton*?'

'You're not? Seeing you and Amanda come out –'

'Out of the Compton?' His voice rasped as he cut across what Martha was saying. It was a deep, vibrant voice and remembering that he was a student, she thought that it would be very useful to him if he ever became a teacher who had to handle large classes. 'Not Amanda and me.'

Amanda put a hand on his sleeve. 'Don – '

'But I'm sure I saw you,' Martha said.

He shook his head. 'As it happens, we met outside the Compton. We didn't go in. I've got a room in a motel.'

Of course Martha knew that it was a lie. She had seen him and Amanda come out of the hotel. But no doubt he had good reasons of his own, or thought that he had, for trying to keep this odd little fact about himself and Amanda a secret. A good many people seemed to feel safer in life if they concealed themselves amongst confusing clouds of lies. Martha's second husband had been a compulsive liar, yet for a time she had most compulsively loved him.

'Well, now you're here, you'll stay and have dinner with us, won't you?' she said. 'You and Amanda have probably a lot to talk over.'

Before he could answer, Mr Syme interrupted.

'Martha, you are forgetting the normal proprieties. You have not introduced these young people to each other. If they are going to be spending the night under the same roof, they should at least become acquainted. Miss Aspinall – Mrs Hassall – Mr Turner.'

He smiled all round. His geniality was astonishing. He was taking the situation much better than Martha had dared to hope. In fact, he was taking it so well that she felt a twinge of uneasiness. Had he been up to something? Had he some card up his sleeve that he would shortly play and that would completely and devastatingly upset the apple-cart?

There was actually a touch of smugness about him at the moment, as if he were really very pleased at the way things were going. Martha remembered the air of welcome with which he had opened the door to her, and the way that his look of pleasure had faded when he had seen that it was only she. Did that mean that he was expecting someone else to come and remove him from this intolerable household? Had the squeak of the gate heralded, he thought, a taxi,

come to collect him and take him off, say, to the comfort
and quiet of his club for the next few nights?

Well, if that was how it was, he could go away and stay
away for as long as he liked. It would make no difference
to Martha. In fact, it would make a nice change. It would
give her a rest.

The garden gate squeaked again.

Mr Syme went hurrying out to the front door.

So she had been right, Martha thought, he had been
expecting rescue. She did not follow him out into the hall.
Sandra, Amanda and Don also stayed where they were,
but Don suddenly put his arm round Amanda and held her
close to him. They seemed both to become even more tense
than they had been a moment before. They had barely
glanced at Sandra. But she was looking at them with deep
interest, watching them in wonderment, almost as if, in
their closeness, their concentration on one another, together
with the sense of hurt in each of them at something that the
other had done, they were members of an unfamiliar
species.

The front door opened.

A woman's voice said, 'Mr Syme?'

Amanda gave a little cry, broke away from Don and
shot into the hall.

'Mummy – oh no!' The shrill words sounded desolate
and hopeless.

'Oh, Amanda, my darling,' the woman's voice said,
'thank God we've found you at last! Last night we went
almost mad with worry. The things we thought of that
could have happened to you! At one in the morning we
telephoned Don, thinking perhaps you were with him, but
he didn't know anything either. So we made up our minds
to go to the police this morning if we didn't hear from you.
But we won't talk about that now. Just get your things and
come away with us. We're staying for the night at the
Compton – '

'The Compton? Oh no. No, I won't – !'

The words ended in a choked little gurgle.

Martha reached the hall just in time to see Amanda slip quietly to the floor in a dead faint.

CHAPTER IV

'It was all your doing, wasn't it, Edward?' Martha said to
Mr Syme half an hour later as she stood by the kitchen
sink, pushing stuffing into the chicken.

Mr Syme was sitting on the sofa, holding a glass of gin
and tonic and wearing a look of sardonic satisfaction on his
smooth, distinguished face. A glass of gin and tonic was on
the draining-board at Martha's elbow. Her visitors' alco-
holic needs had been coped with by setting out a tray of
bottles and glasses in the sitting-room. But no one had yet
come downstairs to make any use of it. So far as Martha
knew, Amanda, her parents and Don Turner were all in
Amanda's room, to which she had walked, with her father's
arm round her, as soon as she had recovered from her faint.

This had been almost immediately. And once in her room
she had refused to lie down, as Martha knew, because she
had taken Amanda's suitcase up after her, intruding for a
moment on the family scene, which had frozen into stillness
as long as she had remained there, but had erupted into
angrily arguing voices as soon as she had withdrawn. Going
downstairs, Martha had heard Amanda's mother insisting
that Amanda should come away immediately to the Compton Hotel, and Amanda, almost screaming, saying that all
she wanted was to be left alone.

By contrast, plump little Sandra Aspinall had been beautifully accommodating. Shown her room, a small room,
opposite Martha's, rather oddly furnished with bits and
pieces for which there had been no possible use anywhere
else, she had expressed delight at its comfort, and had suggested that Martha should give her the sheets for the bed,
so that Sandra herself could make it up without troubling

Martha, who obviously had more than enough on her hands.

When Martha had said that if Sandra wanted a drink, she would find one in the sitting-room, the girl had given a sigh of pleasure, then impulsively had embraced Martha and kissed her. Martha had gone downstairs and had started mixing hot water into the packet of stuffing for the chicken.

A few minutes later Mr Syme had appeared, carefully carrying a drink for each of them, and putting Martha's down beside her, had settled himself comfortably on the rug that covered the old sofa.

'I admit it,' he said. 'That is, I admit I brought Mrs Hassall's parents here. But I disclaim all knowledge of how Mr Turner traced her.'

'But how did you do it?' Martha asked. 'How did you know where to find them?'

He smiled complacently.

'You may remember you tried to persuade her over breakfast to get in touch with them.'

'Yes,' Martha answered. 'You were eavesdropping, were you?'

'I wouldn't describe it as eavesdropping,' he said. 'There appeared to be nothing in the least private about the conversation. You'd even left this door half-open. And I listened only long enough to become sure that you weren't going to achieve your aim. So I went up to Mrs Hassall's room, found her handbag there –'

'Her *handbag*!' Martha broke in violently. She swung round on him. 'Do you mean to say you looked in her *handbag*?'

Her own handbag was enough of an extension of herself for her to feel that for anyone else to look inside it without her permission would be a kind of rape.

'Yes, indeed,' Mr Syme said without any sign of guilt. 'It seemed to me of the highest importance that her parents should know where the girl was. Both for their sake and for hers. And, let me add, for yours. I saw the possibility of a very ugly situation developing, with perhaps the police being called in and tracing her here, and heaven help us, even the television people arriving and asking you impertinent questions as to how you became involved. And about how you felt about it. Have you noticed how they keep asking people what their *feelings* were about quite private matters? Quite idiotic, of course, because who's going to tell them the truth? And it's also in the worst of taste, though I don't suppose that worries them. But perhaps I've frustrated some secret desire of yours to appear on television, Martha my dear. If so, I apologize for that, but not for anything else.'

Martha turned back to the chicken. 'You're a poisonous man, you know,' she said. 'I wonder why I put up with you.'

'Because you need me,' he said. 'Precisely at a time like this, you know how much you depend on me.'

'Luckily we don't have many times like this,' Martha said as she put the chicken into a baking-tin. 'All right, you went snooping in Amanda's handbag. What happened next?'

'I found one or two letters addressed to Mrs Amanda Hassall at an address in St John's Wood. Of course, those weren't much use to me, as her parents' name would not be Hassall. I was intending, you see, if I found their name, to ring Inquiries and ask for their telephone number. However, there was a little address book in her handbag, and one entry was simply a telephone number, jotted down as if she were afraid of forgetting it, whereas the name and address of the person it belonged to were too familiar to need noting down. And the exchange number happened to be the same as that of some friends of mine in St John's Wood. So I simply put two and two together, used the telephone in your bedroom – I do hope you don't mind the intrusion – so that I shouldn't be heard by the two of you down here, and rang the number. A woman answered, saying she was Mrs Gravely. I asked her if by any chance she was the mother of a Mrs Hassall, and I could hear her literally crying, yes, crying for joy, my dear Martha, when I told her where to find her daughter.'

'And her daughter literally fainted when her mother found her,' Martha said. 'I hope you're satisfied with your work. How are you going to feel if you've brought on a miscarriage? – because I shouldn't be at all surprised if that's just what you've done.' She put the chicken into the oven. 'You read the letters in her handbag, I suppose. Were they from Don?'

'I certainly did *not* read the letters,' Mr Syme said sharply. 'I don't read other people's letters.'

'So you do draw the line somewhere. I was beginning to wonder how many of mine you'd read.'

'Now whatever makes you say something as unkind as that?' he demanded. 'You're really a most peculiar woman. We seem to have a relationship of complete trust, you and I, and most of the time you're kindness itself. And then suddenly you go and say something as cruel as that. It knocks the breath out of one. Don't you realize how it hurts? As if I should dream of reading your letters!'

'Perhaps they aren't interesting enough for you,' she said. 'It's years since I had one I'd mind you reading.' She picked up her drink, carried it to a chair, sat down facing him and kicked her shoes off. 'Anyway, I hope you did right, getting hold of the Gravelys. Apart from your hunt in Amanda's handbag, I don't feel happy about it. They both seem very nice when you talk to them, yet Amanda seems so frightened of them that there must be something wrong somewhere.'

'It's probably just her condition,' Mr Syme said.

'Now, honestly, darling, what do you know about things like that?'

There was a knock at the door.

Martha called out, 'Come in!'

Sandra looked into the kitchen.

'Is it all right if I use the phone, Mrs Crayle?' she asked. 'I'd like to phone Derek.'

'Go ahead,' Martha said. 'It's just there beside you.'

Sandra withdrew without bothering to shut the door behind her.

Martha heard the whir of the telephone dial, then there was a pause, then she heard Sandra say in her slightly whining, nasal voice, 'Derek? It's me.'

There was another pause, then Sandra resumed, 'Don't be like that. I'm ringing up just to tell you I'm all right . . . What? . . . Oh, for God's sake! I'm all *right*, I tell you. Only, like I said, I'm not coming back . . . No, there isn't anybody else. Is it likely? So don't start trying to think how you'll murder him or anything. I only rang up so you shouldn't think I'd fallen under a bus. I've got a room for the moment with a very nice lady called Mrs Crayle, who works for the National Guild for the Welfare of Unmarried Mothers and sometimes lets people stay with her . . . Where? Oh, in Helsington. I went home to Hemlow and had a talk with Mr Gorton and he told me where to go . . . What? Can you come to see me? Well, I don't know about that. What'd be the point of it? I don't want you coming here, bothering Mrs Crayle. She's been super. And she's got another girl staying here, a Mrs Hassall, and her boyfriend's turned up and so have her parents, and they're all acting crazy and making scenes and I can tell Mrs Crayle's good and fed up. So don't you come here, making trouble, because I won't stand for it . . . Oh, all right, I'll telephone again sometime and perhaps we can fix up where to meet where we won't be a nuisance to Mrs Crayle or anyone. Not that it'll make any difference, you do understand that, don't you, Derek? I'm not coming back.'

She put the telephone down.

'Well, that's that,' she said, putting her head in at the kitchen door again. 'Now he can have a good night's sleep. Would you believe it, he says he never had a wink of sleep last night? I can just see it? Derek's never worried about anyone but himself. You know, I wouldn't be surprised if it does him good, me walking out on him like this. He's always believed he could make other people, and specially me, do what he wanted. He's a very surprised boy just at the moment, I could tell that.'

She gave a little crow of laughter and left the kitchen again.

'Not someone who's going to be one of life's victims,' Mr Syme observed. 'Two very different temperaments, that girl and Mrs Hassall. They're both what used once to be called unfortunate, but they take their misfortunes in very different ways. Now drink up that drink, Martha, and I'll fetch you another.'

'No thank you,' Martha said. 'Not just yet. I'll peel the potatoes first.'

She slid her feet back into her shoes, stood up and returned to the sink.

Mr Syme left the kitchen to refill his own glass. While Martha counted out into a bowl what she thought would be enough potatoes for the meal ahead and began to peel them. Not that she usually ate potatoes herself nowadays. Ever since she had given up taking boarders she had found it difficult not to put on weight and she tried to fight this by denying herself the things which the diet sheets in the women's magazines told her to avoid. The trouble about that was that what the diet sheets told her to eat was about twice the amount that she ever dreamt of eating normally. She did not like to think just how far she would spread in all directions if she really followed their instructions.

However, Mr Syme liked a good heap of potatoes with his supper, and probably Don Turner, if he stayed, would too, even if the two pregnant young women had been advised to keep off them. So it would be wise not to skimp them.

A slight cough in the doorway made her turn.

Amanda's mother, Mrs Gravely, stood there, hesitant about entering. She was a very small woman with a neat, slender figure, soft blue eyes, a gentle expression and thin, limply curling hair, discreetly touched up with a blue rinse. Her husband also was very short, Martha had noticed. Amanda was several inches taller than either of them. And neither was in the least as Martha had expected from what Amanda had said about them. Mrs Gravely particularly seemed so mild, so shrinking, that it was difficult to imagine why her daughter should have felt that she had to run away from her, and then have fainted at the mere sight of her.

The little woman was probably about the same age as Martha, though she seemed to Martha to be a good many years older than she was herself. Martha felt, in fact, as if Mrs Gravely might almost belong to another generation. But other women often gave Martha that feeling. Even when she was with someone who was years younger than she was, such as Olive Mason, she would often be assailed, absurdly and sometimes most embarrassingly, by a sense of ignorance, inexperience and immaturity.

'You're busy,' Mrs Gravely said in a light, soft voice. 'I don't want to disturb you. But I'd be so grateful if I could have a few minutes' talk with you.'

'If you don't mind my just going on with these . . .' Martha gestured at the potatoes. 'Come in and sit down.'

Mrs Gravely advanced to the sofa and sat down on the edge of it. She sat with her back straight and her feet placed carefully together. She was wearing a grey suède jacket over a grey and red jersey dress, a single string of pearls, small pearl ear-rings, black patent leather shoes, and was carrying a grey, ostrich-skin handbag. All her clothes were good and were even, in a quiet way, smart, and yet there was

something so shy and uneasy about the way that she wore
them that they looked merely presentably neat and uninteresting.

'Of course, you understand, it's her condition,' she said,
unknowingly echoing Mr Syme. 'She isn't like this normally. She's really a quite sensible girl.'

'I'm sure she is,' Martha answered, the potato peeler rip-
ping down the sides of the potatoes.

'You've been so good to her. My husband and I are both
so grateful. So I wanted to explain . . .' There was no depth
in Mrs Gravely's voice. It slid along the surface of the
words, putting no meaning into them. 'In case she's been
telling you some rather strange things, I do want you to
understand they aren't lies. She honestly believes them.'

'If you mean about your trying to get her to have the
child adopted – '

'Oh, no, no, not that. I meant about her husband.'

'Her husband?' Martha put salt into the panful of potatoes and carried it to the gas stove. 'She's hardly spoken
about him. She did tell me he'd left her, but that's about
all.'

'But he didn't, you see.'

Martha turned from the stove to look at the woman on
the sofa. Her mild blue eyes, meeting Martha's, were full of
unhappy apology.

'It was she who left him, do you mean?' Martha said.
'And he won't divorce her? Is that why she can't marry
Don?'

'Oh, no, no,' Mrs Gravely said again. 'When I said that
– that he didn't leave her – I didn't mean anything like
that. I meant, you see, the poor boy is dead.'

'*Dead*?' Martha said in astonishment. 'And she doesn't
know it?'

'Oh, she knows it, yes, of course she does, and she'd never
say anything else if she weren't – weren't a little unbalanced
at the moment. I do hope you understand. I mean that she

hasn't been deliberately telling you lies.'

'Lies don't worry me much, so many people tell them.'
Martha sat down in the chair facing the other woman. 'But
I don't understand at all. What happened?'

'Laurie was killed in an air crash three years ago. That
one over Nairobi – d'you remember it? The poor boy was
going out there to be a teacher. He would have been a
wonderful teacher, he was so full of idealism and enthus-
iasm. And he and Amanda had been married only a few
months and they were madly in love with each other. If
only you could have seen it! They were so radiantly happy,
so – oh so – ' Mrs Gravely's voice shook. She pressed her
small hands tightly together, locking up some intense emotion between them. 'We were so fond of him too, my husband and I. He was such a good-looking boy and so kind
and understanding. Amanda was going to follow him in a
few weeks. And then came the news of the crash – the end
of everything. Such heartbreak. Heartbreak for my husband
and me too, partly because we'd cared so much for Laurie
ourselves, he'd really been one of the family, but also because of watching what Amanda went through. Oh, Mrs
Crayle, it was terrible. She suffered so intensely.'

Martha nodded. 'Yes, I see. She had a breakdown and
wouldn't believe he was dead.'

'Yes. Well, no. Not exactly.'

'But she doesn't believe he's dead.'

'No, not now. But at the beginning she seemed to accept
it. It's only recently, since she started having this baby . . .
That's what I meant when I said it was her condition. It's
only these last few weeks that she's started saying Laurie
left her and isn't dead. We've both been most terribly worried about it, my husband and I. We wanted her to see a
doctor – a psychiatrist, you know, we know such a nice one
– but she wouldn't hear of it. And then when we suggested
– oh, ever so gently – that she might think of having her
child adopted, because truly we were afraid, however much

we helped, that she might not be fit to look after it if she
didn't recover fully from this dreadfully tragic delusion, she
ran away from us. And you know the rest. And indeed,
we're very, very grateful to you for looking after her, and to
that nice Mr Syme for letting us know where she was.'

'Do you know why she came to Helsington?' Martha
asked. 'She says it was because she had some happy holidays
here when she was a child, staying with a grandmother.'

Mrs Gravely put her head on one side in a puzzled way.
'How odd,' she said. 'I don't think she's ever been to Helsington in her life. And I'd be surprised if she remembers
either of her grandmothers. Well, one of them I know she
doesn't. My husband's mother died when he was a child.
And my own died when Amanda was only two or three
years old. I'm sure she can't remember her. Anyway, my
mother lived in Torquay.'

'Then, about Don . . .'

'Oh, Don!' Mrs Gravely exclaimed, her tense little body
giving a sudden bounce on the sofa so that its ancient
springs sang out. 'You mean, how could a nice girl like
Amanda become involved with a boy like that? Well, I've
got a theory about that.' Her eyes brightened as she said it,
as if to have a theory were a very daring thing. 'You see, for
about two years after Laurie's death Amanda had no interest in men at all. She lived with us and she got a job, doing
some translating work for a publisher. She speaks excellent
French and German. It was very poorly paid and I'm sure
it can't have been at all interesting, but we understood that
she liked it because she could do nearly all her work at
home and didn't have to go out and face other people. And
of course it distressed us that she felt like that, but we
thought that if we didn't put any pressure on her she'd get
over it in her own time, and we tried – oh, Mrs Crayle, we
did try so hard – to give her a happy home and help her in
every way we could think of. And then she started going
out a little, and we were so pleased, and then one day, about

six months ago, without any warning, she simply told us she was leaving to go and live with Don, whom she'd never even mentioned before, and she packed up and left.'

'She seems rather given to doing that kind of thing,' Martha said. 'She seems to have left Don all of a sudden a week ago and come back to you. And then yesterday she left you suddenly all over again.'

'Yes, well, she's always been impulsive,' Mrs Gravely agreed.

'But this theory of yours . . .?'

'Oh yes. Well, it's about Don and the way they've been living together without getting married. I don't want you to get a wrong impression of her. She isn't at all a promiscuous girl. It's all Don's fault. Until just recently I think she's always felt they were as good as married. But still, I don't think it's ever been right for her. Underneath she's always felt guilty about it and insecure. Of course, I know their generation doesn't take marriage seriously in the way we did when we were young, but still I think that if Don had been ready to marry her, instead of talking of waiting until he'd got his Ph.D. and so on, she'd never have started imagining she was still married, that Laurie was alive. It stands to reason, doesn't it? If she'd really been happy with Don, she'd never have started imagining all these things about Laurie.'

Martha nodded thoughtfully. She herself had taken two marriages very seriously, but it took two people, unfortunately, to make a marriage serious and she seemed never to have had the art of picking serious men.

'Do you know why she left Don so suddenly?' she asked.

'They had a quarrel,' Mrs Gravely answered. 'She's never told us just what it was about. We never pressed her to tell us anything she didn't want to. We were so glad to have her living at home again, we tried to do everything we could to make her feel welcome.'

'You didn't want her to marry Don?'

'Not really. For the child's sake, yes, of course. But we didn't think that it would last. We didn't think she'd ever be happy with him. He's a rather overbearing type of young man. And she's so gentle. I don't mean I think he actually treated her with violence. But even if he had, Amanda would never have said anything about it. But I've always felt there was something wrong between them. When she came to see us she'd never discuss him with us. She only insisted that she couldn't and wouldn't marry him because Laurie was alive.'

'Did Don come with her when she came to see you?'

'Hardly ever. In the circumstances, we preferred not to invite him.'

'Yet when Mr Syme telephoned you this morning, you let Don know you'd heard and where to find her.' Martha smiled. 'Feeling as you do about him, that was kind.'

'Oh, but we didn't tell him anything. We didn't even think of it.'

'Then how did he find her?'

'I suppose Amanda let him know where she was. In the state she's in, you can see for yourself, she might do anything.'

'I suppose so.'

Martha had heard heavy footsteps approach the kitchen, pause outside the door, then withdraw. The footsteps of Mr Syme, who had decided against entering with his second drink when he had heard Mrs Gravely's voice inside. He had probably returned to the sitting-room. It reminded Martha that she had not yet offered Mrs Gravely a drink, though she was very likely in sore need of one.

'Shall we join the others now?' she suggested. 'The supper can look after itself for the present.'

Mrs Gravely got to her feet. Her hands were still pressed together, keeping a tight hold on some emotion that was almost too much for her. 'Just so long as you understand, Amanda would never mislead you deliberately, that's what

I've been trying to explain.'

'Yes, I know. I do understand. It's a very tragic story.'

Opening the kitchen door, Martha showed Mrs Gravely the way to the sitting-room.

Mr Syme was there with the rest of Martha's curiously assembled houseful of guests. The gas fire had been lit, but the room, as always, felt cold. The chandelier which hung from the centre of the high ceiling and which consisted of a collection of imitation candles, stuck in holders of imitation oak, cast a flat, lifeless light on the too shiny furniture and on the faces of everyone there.

Mr Gravely, standing on the hearthrug, was holding a glass of whisky. Although hardly taller than his wife, he was a heavily built man who gave an impression of intense, formidable energy. He looked as if probably he would always try to sweep difficulties brusquely out of his way rather than waste time discussing them. An intimidating man, Martha thought, although in her short acquaintance with him he had been very quiet, leaving nearly all the talking to his wife. He had black eyes and thick smooth hair that was still as black as it could ever have been in his youth, and he wore a well-cut suit of charcoal grey, a grey and white striped shirt, a pale grey tie and black shoes. He would have been all grey and black and white if it had not been for the shiny pink of his face, a colour heightened perhaps by anger as he gazed with expressionless concentration at his daughter.

She was sitting on one of the velvet-covered chairs, looking lost and alone, as if there were no one else in the room with her. She did not meet her father's gaze, or that of Don Turner, who was standing by the window, his tall reflection mirrored in the big, dark pane behind him. He was nursing a glass of beer, but had not drunk anything from it, and was watching Amanda with a restless kind of anxiety. It might have been that he was terribly afraid that her parents were going to take her away from him again. He looked as if he were almost choking with the effort of holding back words that were boiling up inside him.

Mr Syme had turned on the seven o'clock news on the radio but it was obvious that no one was listening to it except Sandra Aspinall, who was sitting in a chair with her feet drawn up under her. She was sipping at a glass of gin and tonic and was smiling contentedly and rather sleepily at the transistor as it spoke of flood, fire, earthquake and bomb with a detachment that made these daily occurrences of life seem remote and unreal. She looked, if anything, pleased and interested to hear that such things were happening in the world around her when she herself had arranged to be so comfortable and secure.

Martha crossed to the bay-window and drew the ruby red velvet curtains across it. The wind buffeted the glass, and flattened dead leaves from the chestnuts against it. The heavy curtains did not shut out the sound of the wind. It cried eerily down the chimney, in competition with the hissing sound of the gas.

'And now,' the transistor was saying behind her, 'here is a police message. The man who was found shot dead in the Compton Hotel, Helsington, today, has been identified as Mr Leonard Henderson of 19 Hoe Street, London. The police are anxious to interview a young woman, aged twenty-four or five, of medium height, wearing a blue and green tweed coat, with long fair hair, and carrying a small suitcase, who visited the hotel in the afternoon, and who they think may be able to help them with their inquiries.'

CHAPTER V

THE TRANSISTOR went on talking, yet the feeling in the room was one of dead silence. The gold and white wallpaper, the ruby red curtains, the flat, dead light from the chandelier, turned the room into an unnatural tableau, peopled by waxworks.

Then Mr Syme switched the radio off and Don Turner took two swift strides to stand behind Amanda's chair and pressed his hands on her shoulders. It was as if he felt that she had to be stopped from leaping from her chair and running out, or crying out, or simply falling apart in pieces.

She gave no sign of falling apart. She sat rigid and still, contriving not to meet the eyes of anyone in the room. She looked as if she were thinking deeply of some private matter which was no concern of any of the people round her.

Her mother gave a little whimpering cry. 'I don't understand. Why are you all looking at Amanda like that?'

But her face had become very white, as if her mind had leapt ahead of her words.

Her husband said harshly, 'Amanda, what's this all about? Why are all these people looking as if that announcement had something to do with you? Who is this Leonard Henderson?'

Amanda did not answer, but she moved in her chair to escape the pressure of Don Turner's hands. He let them hang at his sides, then thrust them abruptly into his pockets.

'I told you,' he muttered. 'I told you there was no time. You shouldn't have stayed.'

'I don't understand,' Mrs Gravely repeated in a high, thin voice. 'Amanda's got a blue and green coat and long fair hair, but so have lots of other girls. And she doesn't know any Leonard Henderson.'

Amanda still did not look at anyone. Speaking to the wall opposite her, she said, 'There *is* no Leonard Henderson.'

'Of course not, dear,' her mother said. 'That's just what I meant. There's no one you know of that name.'

'No one at all,' Amanda agreed. 'The man they're talking about, you see, is really Laurie. Laurie Hassall – Leonard Henderson – he kept the initials. They often do, I believe, when they change their names.'

Her father went to her side and put a hand on the shoulder where one of Don's hands had rested.

'Amanda, dearest, Laurie's dead. This man, whoever he is – '

As if his touch enraged her, she flung up her head and screamed at him, 'Laurie's alive! I've told you so over and over again. No, no, he's not alive, he's dead. But not till this afternoon. And if you'd believed me, perhaps this wouldn't have happened. But you thought I was mad.'

The ruddiness had faded out of Mr Gravely's face. He looked all ash-coloured now.

'We'll talk about that later,' he said. 'This man who you believe was Laurie, what have you done to him?'

'She's done nothing to anybody,' his wife cried. 'How can you say such a thing?'

'Be quiet, Beryl,' Mr Gravely said. 'Go on, Amanda. We're your family. We love you. We'll help you. But what have you done?'

'You all talk too much,' Don Turner said. 'Why don't you let Amanda tell her story in her own way if she wants to, and if she doesn't, for God's sake, leave her alone.'

'We can hardly leave her alone,' Mr Gravely retorted, 'when any of these people here is liable to go to the telephone at any moment and tell the police that the girl they're looking for is here in this house. As a matter of fact, it's their duty to do so. If they'll wait a little while, however, so that Amanda can tell us, her parents, what's happened, we'll be deeply grateful to them. But if they feel they must act at once, it's not for us to stop them.'

He looked challengingly round the room.

Martha, who was much too absorbed in what was happening to feel in the least like telephoning the police, glanced uneasily at Mr Syme. He was a man who was subject to sharp attacks of a sense of duty, but just how these would affect him was always unpredictable. They might make him suddenly dash off furious letters to newspapers on subjects about which Martha had never realized that he felt strongly, or they might make him perform acts of remarkable kindness to relative strangers, or they might make him perhaps keep utterly silent about something or other when everyone else was talking about it, simply because it had originally been told to him in confidence.

At the moment he was looking very stern and was holding himself with upright dignity, every inch of him a good citizen, preparing to do what he ought. But there was a certain gleam of curiosity in his eyes and in fact, when Mr Gravely looked him hard in the face, Mr Syme merely looked straight through him and said nothing at all. And when Mr Gravely's glance swung round to Sandra Aspinall, curled up in her chair, she made a sound that might have been the beginning of a titter, but clapped a hand over her mouth and held it in.

'Well, Amanda,' Mr Gravely said, 'it seems you are to be given a little time. So tell us how you came to take this man Leonard Henderson for poor Laurie – or to pretend that you did. Because in your heart you've always known Laurie's been dead a long time. Haven't you, dearest? When you stop pretending, you know Laurie's dead.'

'He isn't. He wasn't.' Amanda gave a tired little sigh. 'I've tried to tell you about it so often, but you'd never listen to me. That day in the Underground at Piccadilly last August. We were only a few feet apart and we looked straight at one another, and he looked as if he'd been hit, then he turned and ran. I tried to follow, but I couldn't. There were too many people. I tripped over someone's foot and I fell and when I got up again he was gone. But I knew it was Laurie. He was my husband, you know. I knew him by sight. You'll agree to that, won't you? You won't say I'm mad for thinking I knew his face. I'd hardly mistake someone else for him, would I?'

Mrs Gravely had moved across the room to sit beside her daughter, and laid a delicate little hand on her wrist.

'Laurie died in that plane crash over Nairobi, my darling,' she said. 'They identified the body.'

'They didn't, you know,' Amanda answered. 'You're forgetting. Several of the bodies were so badly burned they were unidentifiable. It was just his luggage they actually identified.'

'But he was on the plane,' Mrs Gravely said. 'We saw him off together, don't you remember? We saw him go out to the plane.'

'We saw him go into the departure lounge. That's quite another thing.'

'Mrs Hassall, a moment,' Mr Syme said suddenly, getting it in just ahead of something that Mr Gravely had been about to say. 'Won't you tell us quite simply what you believe happened that day when your husband was supposed to fly to Nairobi? If he intended to go, why should he have changed his mind at the last moment? If you were happy together, why should he hide from you? You must have explained these things to yourself in some way.'

She nodded. 'Of course. What I believe is, he never intended to go to Nairobi. He only took the job as a blind and always meant to wait in the departure lounge until he knew we'd gone away and then he was going to slip out again and go his own way without me. And about our being happy together – well, we weren't. We hated one another.'

'Oh, my darling girl!' Mrs Gravely cried. 'You know

that isn't true. You adored one another. You were both so happy. Anyone could see that.'

'You saw what you wanted to see,' Amanda replied. 'Laurie was a wonderful con man. He took you in completely. You were half in love with him yourself anyway. You used to cling to him and kiss him and tell him how handsome he was and how lucky I'd been to find such a wonderful husband. But of course you couldn't admit to yourself why you thought all those things. You had to convince yourself that I was the happy one, when really it was you. And I had my pride, so I let you think what you liked. If it delighted you so much to have a wonderful handsome son whom you could gorge on with your love, I was past caring. The only thing I minded was the way Laurie used to laugh at you about it afterwards. I minded him jeering at you, when he'd done everything he could to make you act like a fool.'

The cruel little speech was delivered in the same flat tone as Amanda's earlier remarks, and her eyes, fixed again on the wall opposite, looked almost drowsy.

Mrs Gravely snatched her hand back from her daughter's, and stared at the girl as if she had never seen her before.

'I see, I see,' Mr Syme said. 'That would appear to answer one of my questions. But even if the truth was that you and your husband hated one another, why should he have found it necessary to hide from you all this time? Why did he actually let you think he was dead when divorce courts exist simply to help sort out the problems of married couples like yourselves who happen to hate one another?'

'I expect it amused him,' Amanda answered. 'Of course, when he slipped away, he didn't know the plane was going to crash. He didn't know he was going to be written off as dead. But when it happened, I expect he thought it was the best joke of his life. And he may even have thought I'd get married again and then he could come back and blackmail me for bigamy. Or rather, my father. He's quite rich, you know. He's a partner in Burridge and Wellborn – Unit Trust people. And he minds very, very much about respectability. He wouldn't like to have a daughter arrested.'

'I wouldn't have paid him a penny!' Mr Gravely declared loudly. His grey face had turned ruddy again. 'If any of this was true, if he'd treated you as you say, and I'd come face to face with him, I might have killed him with my own hands. Yes, I might very well have done that. I said I would, didn't I, when you came to us that day and told us you'd seen him at Piccadilly? You were so convincing at first I believed you, and I said if he'd really allowed you to suffer as he had, I'd kill him with my own hands – '

'Don't!' Amanda shrieked at him. Her hands came up to clutch both sides of her face as if she were suddenly in great pain. 'Don't say that ever! He's dead. He's been killed. Don't say what you'd have done if you'd known he was alive.'

'Ah, so that's why you fainted, Mrs Hassall, when your parents arrived here,' Mr Syme said thoughtfully. 'It wasn't just at the fact that they'd tracked you down, as we all supposed, or anything to do with your fear that they might force you to have your child adopted. It was because they said they were staying at the Compton Hotel, where you knew your husband had been shot, and for the moment at least you believed it was your father who must have killed him.'

'And don't you see what that means?' Don Turner broke in swiftly. 'If she actually fainted because she believed her father had killed Hassall, then she didn't do it herself, did she?'

Amanda gave an odd little laugh. 'Only you think I did, don't you, Don, my dear love? And really you think I fainted because I thought my father might have seen me in the place.'

Don did not answer and after a moment withdrew, to

stand, a slim black shape, with his back to the rich red curtains across the window. He looked sullen and distracted.
Then all of a sudden he swung round towards the door and
went out.

'He thinks I did it,' Amanda stated, with a trace of what
might have been sad amusement in her voice. 'And he
thinks he's in love with me too. Isn't it strange?'

Mr Syme did not choose to be sidetracked. He was stead-
ily pursuing some line of thought of his own.

'Mrs Hassall, you have referred to your husband as a con
man,' he said. 'You have spoken as if you believed he'd be
willing to blackmail your father. Were those merely figures
of speech or did you mean them literally? In other words,
were you simply venting a certain spleen against your husband when you spoke like that, or have you any positive
knowledge that he had criminal tendencies?'

'Tendencies!' Amanda exclaimed. 'It was long past the
tendency stage. He *was* a criminal.'

'So you meant just what you said.'

'I did indeed.'

'Then, if you'll allow the question, how did you come to
marry him?'

Mrs Gravely looked up from her contemplation of her
locked hands. 'It's none of it true, you know,' she said in a
low voice. 'You shouldn't trouble the poor child with questions. She's been confused and unbalanced ever since she
started having her child. She wishes the child was Laurie's
instead of that wretched Turner boy's, that's her tragedy.'

'The one thing I'm really thankful for,' Amanda said, 'is
that the child isn't Laurie's. That's the one thing about
which I'm not in the very least confused. Why did I marry
him?' She leant back in her chair, transferring her gaze to
the heavily moulded ceiling, a fantasy of plasterwork in
which thoughts could lose themselves. 'To begin with, I
didn't know what he was. He told me his parents were dead,
and that he'd a degree in mathematics, and that he worked

for an engineering firm and had to do a lot of travelling round the country. And he was very good-looking and he seemed to be very much in love with me, and he always had plenty of money, and we got ourselves a nice little flat, and for a time – yes, for a little while – I was very happy. Does that answer your question?'

Mr Syme nodded. 'Partially. I'm curious about what shattered the dream?'

'Well, when he came home after one of his trips, he nearly always brought me an exciting present,' Amanda said. 'Sometimes it was a bottle of expensive scent, sometimes it was a silk scarf, or a handbag, or jewellery. The jewellery used to puzzle me. It looked so good, I almost thought it was real. But if it had been real, I knew he couldn't have afforded it. And then one day I happened to telephone him at his office. It wasn't about anything important, just that Mother wasn't very well, I think, and that I was going over to cook supper for her and could he get his own. And they told me he'd left his job months ago, in fact had only worked for them for a few weeks. So we had it out that night and he laughed at me and told me not to pretend I hadn't known the truth all along. He said I must've known he'd nicked all those nice presents for me . . .'

She moved her head and looked sombrely into the attentive face of Mr Syme.

'He seemed proud of himself about it and seemed to think I ought to be proud of him too, because he was such a clever fellow, making a good living for us without doing a real job. And I . . . Oh, I was still in love with him and didn't know what to do. I didn't even think of going to the police. And Mummy and Daddy weren't the sort of people I could talk to about anything. And I thought that perhaps, if I tried hard, I could reform him. Think of that! Of course he always promised everything I asked, but he still went away on his trips around the country. But at least he stopped bringing me the presents.'

She gave a quick shudder, as if the thought of those presents, so happily accepted at first, had been one of the
bitterest memories that had been left behind.

'And then,' she went on, 'he suddenly said, if I liked, he'd
really give it all up, if only we could start a new life in
another country. There were too many people here who
knew all about him, he said, who wouldn't let him give up.
And it's true we used to get a lot of odd telephone calls,
which he hated me hearing, and I realized he wasn't working alone. So we started watching the advertisements in
newspapers, and one day we saw there was a job going for
a teacher of mathematics in Nairobi, and he applied for it
with some faked testimonials and he got the job. And I
believed – I nearly believed – that he meant to go straight.
Of course, all he really meant to do was disappear. He
could see the sort of strain I was under, living the kind of
life we were, and he didn't trust me not to break down one
day and tell someone or other all about it. Then the plane
he was supposed to have flown out on to Kenya actually
crashed, which was wonderful for him, because it meant he
was officially dead and I wasn't going to try looking for
him, or let on how glad I was to have got rid of him, or any
of the truth about our life together. Which I didn't. This is
the first time I've talked about it since the day he vanished.'

Mr Syme turned to Mr Gravely.

'It seems to me your daughter tells a remarkably con-
sistent story,' he said. 'Are you and your wife still of the
opinion that it is all an invention?'

The Gravelys looked helplessly at one another.

'If it's true . . .' Mr Gravely muttered. 'If it's true, why
didn't she talk to us about it? She came back to live with
us until she went off with Turner. She could have told us
the truth. She could have let us try to help her. Why didn't
she? We aren't monsters.'

'I didn't want help,' Amanda answered excitedly. 'I
didn't want to talk about any of it. As it was all over, the

only thing I wanted was to forget any of it had ever happened. And I made up my mind not to marry again. Don wanted me to marry him, but I thought no, not again. I'll never pledge my love and trust to anyone again. I buried it all as deep as I could. And then Laurie and I saw each other in Piccadilly. I did see him, you know, it wasn't a fantasy. My being pregnant had nothing to do with it, though Don was sure it had when I told him, and so were my parents. It was Don who made me tell them, because he was afraid I was going mad, and he thought they might know more than he did about what to do about it. Actually I soon wished I'd kept the whole thing to myself. But it was a shock, and I was suddenly frightened, and I had to talk to somebody.'

'Then you came to Helsington, looking for your husband,' Mr Syme said. 'Because I suppose that dead man in the Compton *is* your husband.'

'Oh yes,' Amanda answered. 'Of course.'

'But why Helsington? What brought you?'

'A telephone call a week ago. A voice I didn't know told me to go to the Compton Hotel in Helsington today between three and five and ask for Mr Leonard Henderson. The voice said I'd be wise to go if I wanted to clean up the past. Of course I realized that Leonard Henderson was Laurie, and I supposed that for some reason he wanted to see me. Perhaps he needed money or something. And as it happened, I'd begun to want to see him, because I'd been thinking that Don and I perhaps ought to get married, because of the child. You see, actually knowing Laurie was alive, I couldn't marry Don unless we could arrange a divorce. So I thought if Laurie and I could talk, we might be able to work something out. Anyway, it seemed worth trying.'

Martha broke in, 'But you didn't wait till this afternoon, you arrived yesterday and you came to the Guild for help. What made you do that?'

'Honestly, it was for the reason I told you,' Amanda said. 'As soon as the man on the telephone stopped talking – '

'It was a man's voice, was it?' Mr Syme interrupted.

'Yes, it was a man.'

'But not one you knew. Not your husband's.'

'Oh no, it wasn't Laurie. Well, as soon as he rang off, I decided I'd tell Don what had happened. I decided too I'd tell him the whole truth about Laurie, and that I was going to meet him to see what we could do about a divorce. The only thing I didn't mean to tell Don was where I was meeting Laurie, because I didn't want him coming along with me and the two of them meeting. So when Don got home from the university that evening, I started to tell him about the man on the telephone and everything, and he wouldn't even listen. He wouldn't believe a word I said. And instead of my really telling him anything, we only had a horrible row. So I grabbed a few clothes together and told him we were through and I went off home. I suppose that was stupid. I ought to have been more patient. We've always gone in for having a good many rows, but they don't usually last long. But I'd been in a frantic state ever since that call in the morning, and not being believed, just as I hadn't been believed about that meeting in Piccadilly, was more than I could bear.'

'Oh, I understand that very well,' Martha said. 'The one thing that makes me lose my temper is when someone doesn't believe what I've said. Particularly if it's a lie. I really tell so few, I feel they ought to be believed.'

Amanda ignored the interruption. 'Anyway, I dashed off and planted myself on Mother and Father. But that didn't help much, because they started this thing about having the child adopted, which nearly drove me mad. I saw that the only thing for me to do was to get away for a few days by myself and think things out alone. And of course see Laurie, but without saying a single word more about him to anyone.

So I decided I'd simply come down here a day ahead of the time I'd been told and get a room and stay here quietly while I worked out exactly what I was going to say to him. I mean, just what sort of arrangement I was going to propose, and just how far I'd go in threatening him with exposure if he wouldn't do what I wanted. Then I found it much harder than I expected to get a room here and I thought, why didn't I just go straight to the Compton and get a room there? Only by then I was awfully wet, and I only had a small bag with me, and when I saw the Compton on the other side of the street I saw a very important-looking doorman with a lot of gold braid and medal ribbons in the doorway, and I thought there wasn't a chance they'd give me a room. So I stepped back into a doorway to shelter and there you were – I mean, there was a notice saying "National Guild for the Welfare of Unmarried Mothers," and I actually laughed, it seemed such a perfect answer to my problem. But then when you were so kind to me, Mrs Crayle, it gave me a feeling I was here almost on false pretences. I don't think I told you any downright lies, but I didn't say anything about having come here to meet Laurie, or anything like that.'

'Do you want to tell us any more about that?' Mr Syme asked. 'About whether or not you actually saw him today, and why the police are looking for you this evening.'

'Oh, I saw him,' Amanda said. 'And the police are looking for me because I've spent most of the day hanging about the hotel, sitting in the lounge where I could see the door, and asking every now and then at the desk if a Mr Leonard Henderson hadn't registered for the day yet, and being told he hadn't. Then I thought of asking if they'd a Mr Lawrence Hassall, but of course they said no, and they began to give me some rather odd looks, and naturally they remembered me later, when he was found dead.'

'Amanda!' her mother cried piercingly. 'Are you telling

us you saw him *dead*?'

Amanda nodded slowly. 'Alive *and* dead.'

Mrs Gravely clutched at her wrist again. 'What *do* you mean?'

'Well, he came in while I was sitting in the lounge,' Amanda answered. 'It was a bit after four o'clock, I think. He looked just as he used to, except that he was wearing his hair rather longer and had a little moustache. And I rushed up to him and grabbed his sleeve and said "Laurie!" And he stood still with a look of absolute horror on his face, and he shook my hand off and said, "I don't know you, leave me alone!" and darted for the lift. I just stood there. I didn't know what to do. But somehow I managed to take in that the lift stopped at the fifth floor. I didn't go up straight away. I was too shaken. I went back to the lounge and sat down, and I suppose I looked a bit queer because an old lady asked me if I was all right and started fussing over me. I think I sat there for about ten minutes. Then I thought I could at least go up to the fifth floor without anyone noticing and see if I could find a chambermaid or someone who perhaps would tell me where I could find the man who'd just come up. I know it was a stupid idea. If I'd seen anyone, they'd only have told me to go back and ask at the desk. And the girls at the desk were fed up with me. Anyway, I didn't see anybody, but I did see a door half-open, and there was a man lying on the floor inside, and it was Laurie. And he was dead.' The unnatural control of her voice broke violently. Crouching forward in her chair, she clasped her face between her hands in that gesture of seeming to be in sudden pain, and cried shrilly, 'He was dead, he was dead!'

'Oh dear, oh dear,' Mrs Gravely moaned, 'I don't know what she saw but it wasn't Laurie. She's lived in a dream for so long. This is all imagination, every bit of it.'

'She saw something,' Mr Gravely said harshly. 'Perhaps

the man wasn't Laurie. He said downstairs that he didn't know her. She admits that herself. But she saw something. She blundered into something that I don't like the sound of at all. Perhaps the best thing to do would be to get in touch with the police straight away. Whatever they make of her story, they'll keep her safe, which she may not be if she saw something she wasn't meant to.'

'Amanda,' Martha said, speaking as smoothly as she was able to the shuddering girl, 'you haven't told us where Don comes into all this. He was in our doorway opposite the hotel when I went out to do some shopping. He seemed to be watching the hotel. Then when I was leaving the office a little while later with Sandra I saw you and him come out of the hotel together. He told me I'd been wrong about that and that it hadn't been you. Only I wasn't wrong. So how had he found you, and what was he doing in the hotel?'

'Don doesn't come into this!' the girl cried. 'Leave him out of it.'

The front door bell rang.

Martha jumped up from her chair to answer it, hurrying out to the hall. She heard the heavy tread of Mr Syme behind her as she went, and he was at her elbow as she opened the door.

Two men and a young policewoman stood there. The scent of a winter night and of dead leaves blew into the house from the Avenue. The parked cars had all gone, but a car with its lights on stood at the gate. The men were in plain clothes, but neither of them could have been anything but a policeman. One of them, producing his identification, said, 'We're police officers, and we've information that a Mrs Amanda Hassall is staying here. If she is, we should like her to come to the police station, as we think she may be able to help us with our inquiries.'

'Oh God!' Martha exclaimed. 'Are you arresting her? The poor girl's pregnant. For heaven's sake, be careful what you do.'

'We aren't arresting her,' the detective said. He looked a composed young man and spoke with a stolid sort of courtesy. 'We only want to ask her a few questions. She may have some useful information to give us about the death of a man in the Compton Hotel.'

Mr Syme had reached for the detective's identification and studied it distrustfully before handing it back. 'Information?' he said. 'You said you had information that she was staying here. May I ask how you came by that information?'

The detective hesitated, then replied, 'As a matter of fact, it was a telephone call. Anonymous. A good deal of our information reaches us in the form of anonymous telephone calls. And though a good many of them turn out to be hoaxes or hysteria, we don't ignore them.'

'Well, come in,' Martha said. 'I'm Mrs Crayle. Mrs Hassall's been staying here since yesterday evening. Her parents are here too just now, and so is Mr Turner, her fiancé. Perhaps you should take him along to the police station too. I don't like the idea of her going off with you alone. She's been through a very upsetting experience today, and she's very wrought up, and as I said, she's pregnant. You wouldn't want her to have a miscarriage or anything like that, would you? I really think it would be best if he stayed with her.'

'By all means, if she wishes it,' the detective answered.

But when they looked for Don Turner, he was not to be found. Martha, Mr Syme and one of the detectives went from room to room right through the house and by the end of their search were quite certain that the young man had left.

Martha felt immensely sad as Amanda went quietly away with the young policewoman's hand laid gently on her elbow.

'She doesn't seem to be any better than I was at picking

men,' she said to Mr Syme. 'At the first hint of trouble, he walks out on her.'

'And telephones the police,' Mr Syme said, 'to tell them where to find her.'

She turned on him with a curious look. 'Whatever makes you say that?'

'But who else knew she was here?' Mr Syme asked.

CHAPTER VI

'LORD, what a carry-on!' Sandra said. 'How she talked, that girl. I thought she'd never stop.'

'Getting it off her chest at last,' Martha said, 'and quite time too.'

She, Sandra and Mr Syme had sat down in the kitchen to eat the very over-cooked chicken that had at last been rescued from the oven. In the end there were only the three of them to do it. Amanda had left with the police, Don Turner had vanished and Mr and Mrs Gravely, although offered a meal, had returned to the Compton Hotel.

That meant, Martha thought, that there would be enough chicken left over to be eaten cold next day. That was probably just as well. She had a feeling that tomorrow was likely to be complicated.

'I expect you'd like me to move out in the morning,' Sandra went on. 'You've got enough to worry about without having me around.'

'Please yourself,' Martha answered. 'You aren't in the way, if you want to stay.'

'What I thought is, I'd start looking for a job,' Sandra said. 'Miss Mason thought she might be able to help me find one. But if I could stay here for a day or two, of course it'd be a help. Only I don't want to be a nuisance if you've got the police around, bothering you and all. I suppose they'll be back with a lot more questions, won't they? What d'you think, Mrs Crayle, did she do it?'

Mr Syme replied, 'Whatever any of us thinks, I'm sure it would be wisest for us not to weary ourselves with pointless discussion of the matter. None of us has any more information than Mrs Hassall gave us herself. If the police do in fact return tomorrow to ask us more questions, we shall be able to tell them no more than we did tonight.'

Sandra gave him an uncertain look. She had been giving him uncertain looks ever since she had met him. He seemed to be something outside her experience. She appeared to find it difficult to make up her mind whether he was a straight turn or a comic, and whether it would be more appropriate to respond to him with appreciative giggles or to take him seriously. However, she dropped the subject of the murder, and presently, when she had helped Martha with the washing-up, went off to bed.

Martha gave a great yawn and dropped on to the old sofa, kicking off her shoes and lying down full-length.

'God, I'm tired!' she said. 'I suppose it's age creeping up on me. I don't seem able to take this sort of thing as I should have once.'

'I doubt if exactly this sort of thing has ever happened to you before,' Mr Syme said.

'Oh, I don't know,' she answered. 'I had some fairly weird experiences with some of the boarders. Never actually a murder, but there was that poison-pen writer, remember, and that old woman – she was before your time – who liked setting fire to churches by stuffing rags soaked in paraffin up the organ pipes. I never could make out what she had against churches. She seemed so pious, poor old thing. I was so sorry for her when the police came and took her away. I was really upset. But I didn't cave in as I have tonight. I think what I need, darling, is a good stiff drink.'

'You've had several already,' he warned her.

'That's why I need another.'

He got the whisky bottle from its shelf, poured a generous amount into a glass, added a little water and brought it to her. She propped her head up with a cushion, sipped, then rested the glass on her chest.

'Well, *did* she do it?' she asked.

Mr Syme had also helped himself from the whisky bottle. He sat down in the chair facing her.

'If half of what she told us was true,' he said, 'she had motive and opportunity.'

'Do you think it wasn't true, then?'

'As a matter of fact, I was inclined to think that most of it was.'

'What don't you believe?'

He stroked one of his full, smooth cheeks and pondered.

'It's just that there are a few noticeable holes in her story,' he said. 'Perhaps if the police hadn't arrived when they did, she'd have filled them in. But as you yourself pointed out, she never told us where Don Turner fitted in. She didn't tell us how he could have found out where she'd gone or that she'd be at the Compton in the afternoon. Her parents said they hadn't told him about my telephone call. Incidentally, Martha, what an obnoxious pair. A self-important, bullying type of man and a hysterical fool of a woman.'

Martha frowned. 'There you go, making horrible pronouncements like that when you haven't even tried to understand those two poor people. They were both under a great strain, and nobody shows at their best at a time like that. Of course, they're rather conventional and probably having their daughter go off and live with Don without getting married and have an illegitimate baby has shocked them both to the core, but altogether I thought they were taking it rather well. You could see they love her very much and want to do their best for her.'

'She doesn't seem to think so herself.'

'Well, she's under a great strain too. She isn't thinking clearly. I feel very sorry for them all.'

'As you felt sorry for your poor old lady who set fire to churches. I suppose she was under a great strain too.'

'Of course she was, poor old darling. She'd hardly have done it otherwise, would she?'

'And is Don Turner under a strain? What do your intuitions tell you about that young man?'

She drank some more whisky. 'You shouldn't laugh at me,' she said. 'I know lots more about people than you do. If you take a jaundiced view of everyone, you get a quite unbalanced view of their characters.'

'Whereas yours is superbly balanced. Everyone you meet is as good as gold.'

'No, that isn't fair. I'm often very critical of people. But I do try to understand what's the matter with them, instead of just writing them off as no good, as you do. However, to tell you the truth, I'm not absolutely happy about Don.'

'That's news indeed!'

'I said, don't laugh at me!' She raised herself on an elbow on the sofa and pointed a finger at him. 'Would you be happy about a man who walks out on his girl-friend as soon as he sees she's going to get into trouble with the police? I can't help it, that's made a very unpleasant impression on me. I rather liked him till that happened. I thought he'd had a lot to put up with, living with a girl he thought was crazy, even if, as it happened, he was wrong about that. But he tried to look after her and wanted to marry her, when she wouldn't even listen to him. I thought there must be a lot of good in him. But then, just when she needed him most, he walked out on her. I'm sorry, I don't like that.'

'You realize, of course, he could have committed the murder himself,' Mr Syme said. 'He'd motive and opportunity too.'

She chewed a thumbnail. 'I suppose he had. And he could have had a mysterious telephone call too, couldn't he, telling her where to find Laurie Hassall? And when I saw him in the doorway at the office, I suppose he could have been keeping watch for Laurie to arrive. Only he wouldn't have known him by sight, would he? Unless Amanda had a photograph of him. Yes, she probably had a photograph, so Don could have followed Laurie into the hotel and hung back when he saw Amanda go up to him. But when Laurie pushed her away and she went back to the lounge and got fussed over by the old lady there, Don could have dashed after Laurie and gone up in the lift with him and forced his way into his room after him and shot him, and then . . .' Martha took an excited gulp of her whisky as her story gripped her. 'And then Amanda could have come up and found him there! And that's why he somehow doesn't fit into her story. It's because she's covering up for him.'

'And do remember he's probably the only person who could have telephoned the police to give them that information that they said they'd had about where to find Mrs Hassall. The rest of us never left the room from the time of hearing the announcement on the radio until the police came.'

Martha shook her head. 'Somehow I don't believe that.'

Mr Syme gave a sarcastic laugh. 'I do believe the thought of him doing a thing like that upsets you more than the thought of the two of them conspiring together to commit a murder. You have the strangest moral sense.'

'No, no, of course it doesn't,' she said. 'Well, I mean – no, of course not. But there would be something peculiarly revolting and treacherous about doing a thing like that, wouldn't there? And anyway, how could he know she wouldn't promptly tell the police everything about him, when she knew how he'd let her down? No, I'm certain you're wrong. She must have talked to someone else earlier in the day and told them where she was staying.'

'I admit that's possible,' Mr Syme said.

'Besides,' Martha went on, 'we happen to know Don wasn't the only person who knew where Amanda was.'

He raised his eyebrows. 'We do?'

'Yes, you heard it yourself,' she said. 'You heard Sandra telling her boy-friend on the telephone that she was staying with a Mrs Crayle in Helsington and that there was a Mrs Hassall staying here too. And he could easily have found out my address, because I'm the only Crayle in the telephone directory, and he could have telephoned the police from London.'

'Martha, that's an extremely interesting idea!' Mr Syme exclaimed, a gleam appearing in his chill grey eyes. But almost at once the gleam faded and he shook his head. 'No, unfortunately, it won't do. The announcement on the radio only mentioned a young woman with long fair hair, wearing a blue and green coat. It said nothing about a Mrs Hassall. And Miss Aspinall said nothing about Mrs Hassall's appearance. So how could he have connected the one with the other. Unless – ' He paused. His eyes gleamed more brightly than before. 'Unless the boy-friend knows Amanda Hassall! Unless he and of course the Aspinall girl too are involved in this affair! She almost went out of her way to tell him Mrs Hassall was staying here, didn't she? You might say she made a point of it. Martha, my dear, I believe you have said something extraordinarily intelligent.'

'My God,' Martha said complainingly, 'I do distrust you when you say nice things to me. You never mean them.'

He leant forward and patted her hand. 'I'm about the only person you sometimes do distrust, isn't that the truth? I take it as a good sign. I take it as a sign of the solidity of our relationship. When you're talking to me, you aren't afraid to probe beneath the surface. Some day you may even make up your mind to marry me.'

'Oh, not that again. Not now. Not tonight. I'm far too tired.'

Martha closed her eyes.

One day, she thought, when Mr Syme suggested that she should marry him, as he had been doing once or twice every year for some time now, she would give him the shock of his life and accept him. Except that she was not really so unkind. Poor man, he would never get over it. Not that he was a queer, or anything complicated like that, as she had at first suspected when he came to board in the house. Naturally, that was what one always did suspect nowadays if a man stayed unmarried much after the age, say, of thirty-five. But by now she knew quite a lot about Mr Syme's past, for he had had his attacks of confiding in her, and she knew that women had played at least some part in his life. However, at an early age he had been jilted in some peculiarly catastrophic fashion which had left him with a phobia about marriage. He had only suggested it to Martha because he knew that her attitude to it was not unlike his own. Why he felt impelled to do it at all she had never quite understood, unless it was that it gave him a sense of partial proprietorship, not only in her but in the house and his precious rooms upstairs, without involving him in any responsibility. Actually, she was sure, any change in the relationship between them would have disturbed him deeply.

She went to bed early. Her room was at the back of the house with two tall windows, with small balconies outside them, overlooking the garden. It was a room to which she had brought most of the furniture that she had owned before Aunt Gabrielle had come into her life and as a result it was shabbier than most of the other rooms, but more cheerful. The furniture was in light woods, the curtains had a bright pattern of sunflowers on them, the pictures were prints of Matisse and Cezanne. Nothing in the room had cost much, yet once, in the home that she had briefly shared with Martin's father, she had felt very proud of these things that they had chosen together. Now she hardly ever noticed any of them but merely felt that in a slap-dash way, they were comfortable things to live with.

She meant to read a few chapters of the thriller that she had started yesterday evening, but almost as soon as she started reading the telephone at her bedside rang. It was her younger son, Jonathan, ringing up from, of all places, Rome. All the time that he was talking to her about nothing in particular she was wondering what fantastic sum the call was costing him. But she knew that there was no need for her to worry about that. With a wife as rich as the nice girl whom he had married, he could easily treat himself to the luxury of an occasional long chat with his mother, even from Rome. He and Tilda, he told her, had decided to spend the winter there. It was only after he had rung off that it occurred to Martha that she had said nothing to him about Amanda, unmarried mothers or murder. She had never made a habit of loading her sons with her worries, and the boy had sounded so happy it would have been a pity to spoil it.

She returned to her thriller, read for a little while, then switched the light off and slept soundly.

The police returned in the morning. Mr Syme had already left for the library and Sandra had gone out to buy some newspapers and see if any possible jobs were advertised. Martha had washed up the breakfast things, dusted the sitting-room and plumped up the cushions, so that it looked as unused as usual, had gone upstairs to make her bed, then had gone across the passage to take a look into Sandra's room to see if it needed any attention. She found that the bed was unmade and that Sandra's possessions were scattered carelessly about the room. Earlier, after Sandra had had a bath, Martha had found a grey high-water mark round it. Evidently the girl was not nearly as neat or considerate as Amanda.

Martha was just about to start making the bed when the doorbell rang.

The detective who stood on the doorstep was not the same man who had come the evening before. He was a good deal older, much bigger, more heavily built and on his long lined face he had a look of quietly acquired experience of the oddities of the human race which had left him incapable of astonishment. He had light brown eyes which looked down at Martha with an air of detached friendliness.

'Good morning, Mrs Crayle,' he said. 'Remember me?'

'Why, Mr Ditteridge!' she exclaimed. 'How nice to see you!'

Perhaps it was not the way in which he was accustomed to being greeted by the people whom he had come to question on occasions such as this, for he faintly raised his eyebrows, which perhaps was as near as he ever came to expressing surprise.

'Those organ pipes,' Martha went on. 'The poor old thing. How is she, do you know? Has she got any better? But it's a long time ago, isn't it? You were an Inspector then. I expect you're something much more exalted now.'

'Actually, I'm a Superintendent,' he answered.

'Well, come in, Superintendent, and let's have some coffee,' Martha said.

He stepped into the hall.

'I suppose you know why I've come, Mrs Crayle,' he said.

'About Mrs Hassall.'

'That's right.'

'Well, come into the kitchen – you don't mind the kitchen, do you? It's the warmest room in the house. Actually, there isn't a great deal I can tell you about the poor girl, because I brought her here simply because she looked so wet and miserable and hadn't anywhere else to go. I didn't try to find out anything much about her.' Martha led him into the kitchen and gestured at the sofa. 'Sit down, and I'll make the coffee,' she said. 'I'm just ready for some myself.'

Superintendent Ditteridge sat down on the tartan rug on the sofa and waited until Martha had put a cup of instant coffee into his hands.

'Well now,' he said as she settled down with her own cup, 'will you tell me all you can about Mrs Hassall, even if it isn't much? She talked to us pretty freely, but I'd like to know if you corroborate what she says.'

Martha nodded. 'But may I ask just one thing first? This

man who was shot – was he really her husband? I haven't
been able to make up my mind if she was telling the truth
about that, or if the whole thing was a delusion.'

'He was her husband,' Mr Ditteridge answered. 'His
name was Lawrence Hassall. He's been identified by Mr
and Mrs Gravely as well as by Mrs Hassall herself. But he'd
been going under the name of Leonard Henderson for some
time, and under some other names too. And he did one
sentence for burglary and ought to have done a few more,
but he was a tricky character with good intelligence. He
might have made something of himself if he hadn't been
born naturally crooked. We could never get the evidence on
him. But we've had an idea for some time he was responsible for a number of jobs done in this district in recent
months. They've had his hallmark. He specialized in daylight burglaries, done when the owners of the house were
away. Of course, he'd informed himself about that beforehand. He'd walk up to the door without any concealment,
leaving his car at the gate and carrying a bag, as if he was
a doctor. And while he seemed to be ringing the bell, he'd
be doing a quick job of smashing the lock. He went for
jewellery, never anything else. You'd have been safe to leave
as much Georgian silver around as you liked, he wouldn't
have touched it. He didn't take anything that wouldn't go
into that doctor's bag.'

'Was it in his room when they found him?' Martha
asked.

'The bag was,' Mr Ditteridge answered, 'but it was
empty.'

'Then he hadn't stolen anything yet.'

'Or he'd handed the stuff on already to one of his friends.
Or perhaps his murderer took it.'

'Amanda?'

'That's jumping ahead. I should add, however, there
hasn't been a report of a theft this last day or two, so perhaps you're right, he hadn't done the job yet.'

'Who are these friends of his?'

'Just some well-trained associates. Not always the same ones. But they get rid of the stuff for him and can generally line up a slick alibi. Except that once, we've never caught him with anything incriminating on him. But now, if you'd tell me what you know about Mrs Hassall it might help us. In any case, Mrs Crayle, with your permission, I'd like to start my men searching the house. There are a couple of them outside in the car. I'll call them in now. I just thought I'd give you a word of explanation before I set them to work. It isn't only a case of the jewellery, there's the weapon too. It wasn't left behind with the body.'

'I see, yes,' Martha said. 'All right, go ahead.'

He went out to the door and signalled to the two uniformed men in the car at the gate to come in.

Some children, having noticed the car and its occupants, had collected round it, hoping to be witnesses of some drama that might compete with television. They lingered hopefully as the two policemen came up the path to the house, but turned away, disappointed, as they saw Mrs Crayle give the men a friendly greeting and welcome them in. Martha showed the two men the room in which Amanda had slept, told them that they were welcome to search wherever else they liked, then returned to her cooling coffee in the kitchen and started to tell the Superintendent everything that she could remember of her first meeting with Amanda Hassall.

She also told him all that she could remember of what Amanda had said and done in this house, and of the brief glimpse of her that Martha had had when Amanda had come out of the Compton Hotel, to be rushed off down the street by Don Turner.

Mr Ditteridge was very interested in Don Turner. He took Martha a second time over everything that she had to tell him about him.

At the end Mr Ditteridge said with a certain weariness,

'It's a pity about him. He would make a first-class suspect if he hadn't what looks like an unbreakable alibi.'

'But has he?' Martha said. 'I saw him when I went downstairs from the office to do my shopping, and he was there when I got back, but in between he'd have had time to pop into the hotel and do the shooting. If that was when it happened. Do you know exactly when it happened, Mr Ditteridge?'

'It seems it was done just about when Mrs Hassall says it was,' he answered. 'That's to say, some time after four o'clock. A chambermaid passed the room about four-twenty. She saw the door open, went to close it and saw the body inside. And the girl at the desk remembers Hassall coming into the hotel around four o'clock. But you aren't the only person who saw Turner waiting in your doorway for quite a long time, Mrs Crayle. He attracted the attention of the hotel doorman, who didn't much like the way he was standing there, watching the hotel. So he kept an eye on him, and he's prepared to swear Turner never moved from the spot for at least an hour. Turner only left it when he saw Mrs Hassall come out of the hotel. He dashed across the street then and called out to her. But as soon as she saw him she darted back inside, obviously wanting to avoid him. But he followed her, caught up with her, grabbed her by the arm and made a scene that was noticed by several people. They then left together, which I assume was when you saw them. So even if Turner had a motive for murdering Hassall, and he had a pretty good one – revenge for what he'd done to the girl, or perhaps jealousy because the man seemed to matter so much to her – there's not much possibility that Turner did the actual shooting.'

He stood up, tall and solid but slightly stooping, as if he were accustomed to having to bend his head as he went through doorways.

'That's about all, then,' he said. 'Thank you for your help – and the coffee. I remember you were very helpful

over that case of arson. You managed to get the old thing to
go quietly with us, which saved a lot of trouble.'

He started towards the door. But just as he reached it, he
paused.

'No, there's one thing more. Something in what you told
me about your first meeting with Mrs Hassall. She came to
your office the day before yesterday, you said. You sat her
down by the fire and made her some tea. Did you do it in
the office, or did you go into some kind of kitchen?'

Martha was puzzled. 'There's a sort of little scullery opening out of the office. I made the tea in there.'

'So for a few minutes she was alone in the office?'

'Yes.'

'Could you see what she was doing?'

'No.'

'And she hasn't been back to the office since?'

Martha shook her head. 'But I don't understand . . .'

'It's just that we don't know that she hadn't already met
Hassall when she first appeared. I agree it doesn't seem
likely, but we don't know for certain she hasn't been working with him at least recently. His crookedness may have
had nothing to do with why the marriage broke up, and a
professional association may have got started. She's a very
innocent-seeming young woman, and that may have been
very useful to Hassall. So it isn't impossible she was carrying
some loot for him which she concealed somewhere in that
office while you were making the tea. Anyway, I'm rather
anxious to check all the movements of that young woman
from the time she left her parents' home that morning. So
this afternoon I think we'll make a thorough search of the
premises of the National Guild for the Welfare of Unmarried Mothers.'

CHAPTER VII

MARTHA was appalled. Several things struck her all at once. One was that Olive Mason might not have heard anything about the murder. At most she might have heard the radio announcement that a man had been found dead in the Compton Hotel. But there was no reason why she should know of Amanda Hassall's involvement in the murder, or indeed of Amanda Hassall's existence. Further, the fact that Amanda had come to the office, looking for help, and that Martha had taken her home with her, was something that she happened not to have mentioned to Olive.

But if the police were going to descend on the office in the afternoon, to search for some hypothetical jewels, she would have to be forewarned. And Martha would have to grovel suitably, because there was no doubt about it, it was entirely her fault that the Unmarried Mothers had got mixed up in the horrid affair at all.

When Mr Ditteridge had gone, she stayed in the kitchen, thinking. She could hear the two men who had remained in the house moving about overhead. The sound grated on her nerves. She felt sure that they would find nothing of interest, unless perhaps they stumbled on some deep secret of Mr Syme's. He seemed to Martha much the most likely person in the house to have a few deep secrets. And later she would have to grovel to him too about having let the police in, and knowing how he detested having any of his belongings touched, even for the innocent reason of flicking a duster round them, she thought that he was unlikely to take her apologies as well as Olive probably would.

Olive was a very rational individual. She would understand, at least Martha a little desperately hoped that she would, that everything that Martha had done had been with the very best of intentions.

Sighing, Martha got up and went to the telephone. She dialled the number of the office, in case Olive had felt well enough this morning to go back to work. But when there was no answer Martha dialled the number of Olive's flat, and almost at once heard Olive reply, though her normally crisp voice was still thick with her cold.

'Hallo, Olive,' Martha said. 'It's Martha. How are you today?'

'Nice of you to ask,' Olive answered. 'Fact is, though, I'm feeling bloody awful. I was going to ring up to ask if you could carry on on your own. If any real bastard of a problem crops up, you can give me a ring, or save it up for Althea. She'll be home to morrow.'

'I'm afraid a problem's cropped up already,' Martha said. 'That's why I rang. Olive, if you don't mind, I'm coming round to see you. It's very important and it's a bit long and complicated to tell you about on the phone.'

'Oh lord, can't it wait?' Olive groaned. 'I can't think of anything more important than this ruddy head of mine. I've lost count of the aspirins I've taken, but they just don't shift it. I know I ought not to have gone to the office yesterday, I ought to have stayed in bed. Silly of me, but I get so bored here all by myself. But I'm not even dressed and the place is in a bloody mess. I don't feel a damned bit like seeing anybody.'

'I'm awfully sorry you're feeling so bad,' Martha said, 'but this is something quite out of the ordinary. I just don't feel I can handle it on my own. The fact is, the police are going to the office this afternoon – '

'The *police*?' Olive interrupted in a husky squeak. 'Good God, what's happened? Is it something to do with one of the girls? Not a suicide or anything like that?'

'Not a suicide, no.'

'Last time we had the police in it was about a suicide. A horrible business. Upset me for days.'

'Actually this is to do with the murder in the Compton.'

'What murder?'

'Didn't you hear about it on the radio? A man was shot in the Compton yesterday. And the police want to go to the office and – well, make certain investigations.'

There was silence on the line. Then there was the sound of a cough, followed by some throat-clearing. When Olive spoke it was in something like her normal voice, hoarse but brisk. 'All right, come along. But it sounds as if I'd better get dressed and get over to the office presently. If the police are going to be pottering around the place, I'd better be there. But a *murder* – whatever do they think we can tell them about that?'

She rang off.

Martha also put the telephone down, then went upstairs, looking for the two policemen.

She found them in one of the unused bedrooms, one of them going rapidly through the empty drawers of the dressing-table, the other standing on a chair, feeling about on top of the wardrobe.

'I've got to go out,' Martha said. 'If you've finished before I get back, will you let the latch go on the door when you leave?'

Mr Syme always said she was much too casual about letting people such as the window-cleaner or the man who came to read the gas-meter wander about the house on their own, but he could hardly object to her leaving it in the hands of the police.

'Will do,' the man on the chair answered. His hands, as he stepped down from it, showed that he had found nothing on top of the wardrobe but dust.

'And make yourselves tea or coffee, if you like – you'll find all the doings in the kitchen,' she said. 'I'm sorry I have to leave you, but it's important.'

'That's all right,' he said. 'Don't worry. We'll leave everything tidy and lock up behind us.'

'Thank you so much.'

She went to her room, which from minor readjustments on her dressing-table she judged had already been searched, put on her coat and headscarf and started out for Olive Mason's flat.

It was about ten minutes' walk away, on the third floor of a block of flats built about the beginning of the century, in a square at one end of the High Street. All round the square the buildings were of dark red brick, with bay windows and small stone balconies. There was a railed-off garden in the centre of the square, containing some sycamores and some tired-looking holly bushes that never bore any berries. Only in spring it became gay with mauve and white crocuses and the singing of blackbirds. Inside the buildings the flats were mildly but not too depressingly shabby. In fact, Jessell Square was just the kind of place that seemed right for Olive, not up to date, not at all smart, but neat and plain and tolerably comfortable.

Olive's door was open when Martha reached the landing and Olive herself was in the doorway. She was muffled up in a sheepskin jacket, buttoned up to her chin and had a black knitted hood on her head. She looked pale and ill and cross.

Martha exclaimed, 'Oh, Olive, you aren't going out! You're looking dreadful. You ought to be in bed.'

Olive pulled her door shut behind her.

'No, from the little you told me, I thought I'd better get to the office this afternoon,' she said. 'I don't want the police rooting around in our files without me there to keep an eye on them. Those files are confidential. Anyway, I've got to face up to going out some time to do some shopping. There's next to nothing left to eat in the flat.'

'Oh, I could have done the shopping for you, if you'd told me what you wanted,' Martha said. 'Silly of me not to have thought of it when we were phoning. I could have brought the stuff along with me. Do go back to bed, Olive.

You really oughtn't to be up and about.'

Her arguing was automatic. She had worked with Olive
long enough to know that if she had made up her mind to
go to the office that afternoon nothing that Martha could
say would have any effect on her.

'A breath of air won't do me any harm,' Olive said as she
started down the stairs. 'Let's go to the Mariners and have
a drink and sandwiches. I couldn't manage a real meal, but
I ought to eat something, I suppose.'

The Three Mariners was the pub near the office where
Olive and Martha occasionally had a drink together at the
end of the day's work. If they met for lunch it was generally at a café in the High Street, where they could have a
three-course meal which, if remarkably dull, was substan-
tial enough, so Olive said, for her not to need to do more
than boil herself an egg in the evening.

Martha was glad today to have only sandwiches. Nervous
stress had given her a slight feeling of nausea. She was glad
too that Olive was not inclined to talk. Usually she was
not a good listener, for she could never resist breaking
in on anything that was being said to her with strings of
staccato questions. Althea Furnas was much easier to talk
to. She was a mild, quiet, easy-going woman, whose friendly
vagueness only disappeared when it came to fund-raising.
Then, in her gentle way, she seemed to become possessed.
Her pertinacity could be like water wearing away stone.
But her absent-minded poise would not be in the least upset
by the presence of police in her office.

In the Three Mariners Martha and Olive ordered ham
sandwiches, a rum and lemon for Olive and a lager for
Martha. The lounge bar was small and at that hour of the
day not very warm. At some distant date an effort had been
made to smarten it up with red plastic chairs, red-topped
tables, a few fake beams in the ceiling and some horse-
brasses on the walls. But except when it was full, with the
fire burning well and a cheerful elderly waiter coming and

going, it was a rather forbidding little place, not just the best background in the world for confidences. But at least there was some virtue in the fact, Martha thought, that there was no one there yet but herself and Olive.

'I know the whole thing is my fault,' Martha said. 'I do realize that and I'm terribly sorry about it. I ought never to have taken the responsibility on myself that I did without phoning you about it first. And if I'd done that you'd have pointed out that we knew nothing about the *bona fides* of this girl they were looking for, and – '

'What girl?' Olive interrupted.

'I'm sorry, I'm telling it awfully badly,' Martha said. 'It began the day before yesterday, about five o'clock. There was a knock at the door . . .'

She went on to tell Olive about the appearance of Amanda Hassall, and all that had followed.

At first Olive did not seem very interested. She only shook her head and muttered irritably, when Martha told her how casually she had invited Amanda to her home, that Martha should know that that wasn't the policy of the Guild.

It was when Martha mentioned Don Turner that Olive became more peremptory.

'But, Christ, Martha,' she said, 'you mean all this had happened and you never even thought of telling me about it next day. I was there in the office, I asked you if you could take the Aspinall girl in and you said you could and that was a great help, I appreciated it and I said so, didn't I? Well, wouldn't it have been the natural thing to tell me then you'd already got this other girl staying with you? I don't understand why you didn't.'

'It was my bad conscience,' Martha answered. 'I simply didn't want you to know I'd taken her home without consulting you. I know our sort of organization can't function on sudden impulses, and an impulse was all I'd had. And I thought if I didn't say anything about her she could just

stay my own private problem and not get mixed up with the
Guild at all.'

'Is that really all it was?'

'What do you mean?'

'You hadn't found out something about her by then that
was scaring you a bit more than you're letting on to me
now?'

'Well, yes and no. Mr Syme was sure she'd lied about her
real reason for coming to Helsington, and I wasn't as easy
in my mind about her as I'd have liked to be. But I didn't
know anything more about her than she'd told me. Even
when I saw her boy-friend in the doorway downstairs, I
couldn't know he'd anything to do with her. Actually, I
wondered if he was a private detective, watching the people
going in and out of the Compton.'

Olive frowned. 'When was this? You skip about so. Was
this when you were taking her home?'

'No, next day. Yesterday. When I went out to get your
prescription.'

'He was downstairs?'

'Yes, in the street doorway.'

'Watching the hotel?'

'Yes.'

'Where is he now?'

'I don't know. He did a bolt while Amanda was telling us
about the murder. But lots happened before that.' Martha
went back to describing how she had found Don Turner
still in the doorway below when she had returned from her
shopping expedition, and then how she had seen him yet
once more coming out of the Compton Hotel with Amanda.

Olive sat huddled in her sheepskin coat, looking morose
and puzzled. She ate only one of her sandwiches, but decided on a second rum and lemon.

Presently she said, 'I think I begin to understand the
situation and I'm glad you made up your mind to let me in

on your secrets at last, because I'll tell you one thing, Martha, I don't believe for a moment your friend Mr Ditteridge is coming to the office looking for stolen jewellery.'

'What's he coming for then?' Martha asked.

'Just to find out a bit more about us, I imagine. To find out if we're what we make ourselves out to be. And perhaps to see if the way that girl came to us was as much by chance as she's made out.'

'Well, coincidences happen all the time, don't they?' Martha said. 'The weirdest things.'

'Of course they do. And I expect the police get bored as hell tracking down whether they're genuine or not. It must waste a lot of their time. But when there's been a murder, I don't suppose they can take anything on trust.'

'Really, I think this *is* genuine,' Martha said. 'There's nothing so fantastic about it, after all.'

'And it was just the girl's good luck she tried keeping a look-out for her husband from the doorstep of the Unmarried Mothers', where she found someone to take her in for the night?' Olive's tone was sceptical. But she added, 'You may be right.'

'Oh, she may have known we were there and been coming to see us anyway, though I don't see why she should pretend she wasn't if she was,' Martha said. 'The real coincidence is that we happen to be just opposite to the Compton, where she'd been told she'd find this man, Laurie Hassall.'

'That's true. At least, it's true if what she told you about that telephone call and all the rest of it is true. Now we'd better be getting along to the office, hadn't we? We don't want your Mr Ditteridge thinking we're conspiring together suspiciously about anything, do we?'

Olive pulled on the knitted hood that she had pushed back when they had settled down to their lunch and the two of them started out along the windy street, past the medical supply stores, to the office.

Superintendent Ditteridge arrived about half an hour later. He had a sergeant and a constable with him, who, with Olive's reluctant agreement, started a search of the office. But it was a perfunctory business compared with the search of Martha's house and she soon decided that Olive had been right and that what the Superintendent wanted was a talk with Olive herself. He asked her a number of questions about the running of the Guild, about the procedure normally followed when it was decided to help some particular girl, and about how much Olive knew about Amanda Hassall.

Olive answered directly enough so long as his questions were about the Guild, but she became evasive when it came to Amanda. Partly it seemed to be because she herself was puzzled, but also Martha understood that Olive wanted neither to suggest that she had known anything about the girl, nor yet to put too much blame on Martha for having taken up the case without permission. Olive was the sort of person who would always be loyal to a subordinate. Nevertheless, Martha thought that Mr Ditteridge understood the position fairly thoroughly and realized that it was only Martha herself, and not the Guild, that had got entangled in Amanda's affairs.

When he and the other two men had left, Olive said, 'So that's that. Althea's going to laugh like hell when she hears about it, isn't she? The Guild being suspected of being receivers of stolen property — because that's what it comes to, isn't it?' She gave a titter that turned into a fit of coughing. 'We'd be a bloody sight richer than we are if we were. I wish Althea'd been here. She'd have handled it all a lot better than me.'

'But did you notice something a bit odd, Olive?' Martha said. She went to the window of her little office and stood gazing across the street at the flat concrete face of the Compton Hotel. 'The way Mr Ditteridge stood here, I mean, while he was talking. Most of the time while those

other two men were hunting around, he just stood here,
looking out and tossing off the occasional question. I wonder
if one can see the room where it happened from here.'

Olive came to Martha's side and looked out of the window.

The hotel, which Martha had hardly thought about until
today, seemed to her all of a sudden to have acquired some
new quality, secretive and sinister.

'I shouldn't be surprised,' Olive said. 'My own window
faces the other way, and anyway, I think I was at my typewriter all the afternoon, so I didn't see anything. But there's
Sandra. I wonder if she saw anything.'

'I remember she was restless and kept wandering about
and looking out of the window,' Martha said. 'But she
hasn't said anything about having seen anything dramatic
going on over there.'

'How are you getting on with her, incidentally?' Olive
asked.

'Oh, she's no trouble,' Martha answered. 'I haven't seen
her since breakfast. She went out to look for a job.'

'Good. I'll take her off your hands as soon as I can. Now
I'm going home. And I hope you can cope on your own
with any problems that arise, because when I get in I'm
going to take a handful of aspirins and go back to bed and
I don't mean even to answer the telephone, if it rings.'

'What about that shopping you were going to do?' Martha asked. 'Are you sure I can't do it for you?'

'No need to, thanks all the same. I'll just pick up something frozen I can pop into the oven.' Olive put on her hood
again and buttoned her sheepskin jacket up to her chin.
'Give me a ring in the morning and tell me if there's been
any more excitement.'

She went out, leaving Martha uncertain whether Olive
expected her to remain in the office for the usual time or
close it and go home herself.

She decided to stay. She added an inch to her knitting,

answered a few telephone calls, made some tea, and had a brief chat with a psychiatric social worker who dropped in to discuss one of her cases with Olive, but who did not stay long when she found that Olive was not there.

Left alone again, Martha began to brood, not on the murder or on any of the problems that had harassed her all day, but on another one which she had never brought herself to face since the death of Aunt Gabrielle.

It was the problem of why she could not convince herself that she was not a poor woman any longer. If she were to sell that big, empty and actually rather depressing house in Blaydon Avenue she would get a lot of money for it, and if she added that to the fifty thousand pounds that Aunt Gabrielle had left her, she would be what she herself would regard as very rich indeed. She could buy herself a nice, smart little cottage, easy to run, in some pretty village, with a spare bedroom for when the boys came visiting, and she could buy a car and some good clothes and go abroad for her holidays and lead a much more colourful life than she was doing at present. And surely the sooner she got on with doing it, the better, because the older she got, the harder she would find it to face the upheaval.

Only what would then become of Mr Syme?

She smiled to herself as she considered the question. Was it possible that she was going on living as she was just for the sake of the companionship of that rather pompous, rather selfish man? But a man, one should never forget, who had a heart of gold, and who, after his fashion, had stuck to her for ten years. No one in her life had been as faithful to her as Mr Syme.

Except, of course, her sons. They were dear, affectionate boys, who never forgot her for long. And she had other friends too in this rather drab, unassuming little town. But the strangely close, long-lasting relationship that she had had with Mr Syme was unique in her life. She might very much regret disturbing it. And really she was very well off in Helsington, whereas in the very smartest of cottages, wearing the very best of clothes in some strange village, she might be horribly lonely.

By the time that five o'clock arrived and she decided to close up the office and go home, she had reached the state, not unfamiliar to her, of counting her blessings. She was in a composed and cheerful state of mind as she walked homewards, her feet slithering on the rotting leaves on the pavements, and went up the path to the front door and let herself into the house.

So far as she could tell, it was empty. Although it was dusk, no lights had been turned on and the place was silent.

Turning on the hall light, she went upstairs to her room, took off her coat, then deciding that she was tired of the trouser suit that she had been wearing all day, changed into a long, comfortable dress of light wool, vividly patterned in big cartwheels of coral and black. Then she sat down at her dressing-table and gave her short, stiff hair a good brushing.

She had just realized that she was feeling very tired and wished that there was no need for her to get supper for anyone. However, cold chicken, salad and cheese would not be a great deal of trouble. She stood up and went out on to the landing.

There, through the open door just across the passage of the room in which Sandra had slept, she saw in the shadows Sandra's unmade bed.

Martha remembered that she had been about to make the bed when the police had arrived that morning. She went into the room now, turned on the light and pulled the bedclothes back. An unmade bed happened to be for her a symbol of utter squalor. There were all kinds of other untidiness that she could put up with quite easily, but for some reason she could not stand tumbled bedclothes. Bending over the bed, she started deftly straightening and tucking in the sheets.

As she did so, she chanced to glance in the mirror on the wall facing her.

She saw the door behind her open a little way. She saw a shadowy figure on the landing outside. She saw a hand come up with a gun in it. Then, as she flung herself to the floor, she felt a violent pain in her shoulder and heard her own voice screaming wildly.

CHAPTER VIII

SHE HEARD two shots.

The strange thing was that she seemed to hear them after she had started screaming. It took her a moment, coming out of a state of shock, to realize that that was indeed what she had done.

Neither of the shots had gone into her. The pain in her shoulder came from her having wrenched it as she threw herself down. It was a very unreliable shoulder at the best of times. At the age of ten she had fallen off a bicycle, broken a collarbone and torn the muscles, and ever since, if she made certain incautious movements, or sometimes even if she was tired or nervous, the wretched thing started hurting.

Sitting on the floor, rubbing the sharply aching shoulder, she looked around her and tried to take in what had happened.

The figure of which she had caught a glimpse on the landing was gone. Her breathing began to slow down to normal once she was sure of that. But the mirror on the far side of the bed was shattered, and there was a round hole in the plaster of the wall behind it. She could not see where the second bullet had gone, though she was sure that she had heard two shots. Then she saw that some plaster had been chipped away from the cornice above, and she supposed that the bullet must be lodged up there.

Not a very good marksman, her attacker, she reflected thankfully.

But perhaps her screams, taking him by surprise just before he fired, had upset his aim. And so far, at least, it did not seem to have occurred to him to come back to make a proper job of finishing her off.

Of course, he might still be in the house. He might reappear at any moment. Martha felt extremely frightened,
and like the animal that freezes into stillness when danger
threatens, she remained where she was, motionless except
for the unthinking rubbing of her shoulder.

But after a minute or two she recognized the pointlessness
of this and got to her feet. Her legs felt shaky, but she went
to the door and looked out. The landing was dark and
silent. A cold draught seemed to be coming from somewhere,
but she could not be sure that the feeling of chill was not in
herself. Turning back into the room, she finished making
Sandra's bed. As she did so, she looked at the broken
mirror. Was it possible, she wondered, that the would-be
killer had shot at her reflection, and it was that that had
saved her life? But who wanted to take her life? In the
whole wide world, what enemy had she?

It took some courage to leave the room and face the
empty house again. On the landing that peculiar cold
draught was still blowing. There was an eeriness about it
that scared her. Normally there was no draught to speak of
on that landing. Something about it felt unnatural.

Then as soon as she reached the top of the stairs, she
saw where the chill was coming from. It was quite simple.
The front door was wide open.

Moving cautiously step by step, she started down towards
it.

At that moment a figure moved from the darkness outside into the doorway. Another scream rose in her throat.
But before the sound burst from her, she clapped a hand
over her mouth and stood still, simply staring.

She had never seen the man before. He was of medium
height and stockily built, with bulging shoulder muscles,
long arms and a round head that seemed to rest on his
shoulders with hardly any neck. He looked about twenty-
five, and had a round, pallid face with small, bright eyes
under curiously heavy lids, a plump chin and a small mouth

with puckered, protuberant lips. His hair was fair and wavy and curled loosely round his collar. He was wearing a suede jacket which hung open, showing a brilliantly printed shirt, and narrow tan trousers. Martha found none of this reassuring. She had not taken in how the figure on the landing had been dressed. She had only been aware of a strange, slab-like face that had not looked human, the sort of face that she had sometimes seen on television, when villains appeared with nylon stockings over their heads. But a nylon stocking could have been whipped off in an instant and tucked into the pocket of that suede jacket.

She did not come any farther down the stairs.

'Who are you?' she demanded.

'Are you Mrs Crayle?' he asked her back.

'Yes. What do you want?'

'Can I come in?'

'Tell me who you are and what you want.'

'Oh, sorry. I'm Derek Coombes. And I'm looking for Sandra. Sandra Aspinall. She said she was staying here.'

Martha descended a few steps, then paused again.

'Did you find that door like that, or did you open it?' she asked.

'I found it like that. As a matter of fact, I was just going to ring the bell when you showed. I startled you, didn't I? I'm sorry.'

'How long had you been standing there before you decided to ring?'

'Just a moment.'

'Are you sure?'

'Truly.'

'Did you see anyone come out of the door before you reached it?'

'No. Look, what's the trouble? You're in quite a state about something.' He stepped inside the door and began to close it behind him.

'No, wait!' Martha went running down the stairs to

make sure that the door remained open with the light inside shining out into the street, so that any passer-by could see what was going forward in the house. 'Did you see anyone come out of the garden as you came up to the house?'

'No.'

'How did you come?'

'Along the street.'

'I meant, did you come by car or did you walk?'

'I walked from the bus-stop. Look, I wish you'd tell me – '

'Did you see a car drive away as you got near?'

'I didn't see a thing.'

'Then he must be still in the house or the garden!'

The young man's puckered little mouth stretched surprisingly in a wide grin. Perhaps he meant it to be friendly and reassuring, but it only filled Martha with a wild distrust of him.

'You've had an intruder, is that it? It wasn't me, Mrs Crayle. But I can see how you'd be worried, me turning up like this straight afterwards. Well, if you're all alone here and don't like letting in a stranger, I can go away and come back some other time. All I want is to see Sandra.'

Enlightenment suddenly came to Martha.

'All *he* wanted was to see Sandra! It was Sandra he was shooting at! That's why he didn't come back.'

Something all wrong happened to the young man's face then. It ought to have shown incomprehension, shock, surprise. But what it showed was anger and suspicion, which made him look threatening and dangerous.

'Now see here,' he said, reaching out to grab Martha's wrist, 'if anyone's got after Sandra – '

She dodged him and sped up a few stairs till she was above him again.

'Don't touch me!'

At that moment she heard the squeak of the garden gate.

The sound was followed by footsteps tramping up the garden path and Mr Syme appeared in the doorway.

He looked at Derek Coombes and said with a sigh, 'More visitors! Has this gentleman come to stay too? Is he perhaps an Unmarried Father? Are we extending our hospitality to such people now? And how many murders has he got himself involved in?'

The sober voice, the tall, portly presence, were immensely reassuring to Martha, but they seemed to fill Derek Coombes with apprehension.

He said diffidently, 'I'm sorry, I seem to have blundered into something. I just came looking for Sandra, that's all. I had a phone call from her yesterday, telling me she was staying here. And I want to see her. She's my girl-friend, and besides that – well, there are reasons I want to see her. But when I got here the door was wide open and the light was on inside and there was no one about. And then, just as I was going to ring, this lady appeared on the stairs and I'm afraid seeing me scared her because she'd just had a shock of some kind, and she's been talking about an intruder and someone shooting.'

Martha returned downstairs once more, put her arms round Mr Syme's neck and held on to him tightly. He could not quite hide his surprise, but she needed the feeling of the comfortable well-padded solidity of his heavy body.

'It's quite true,' she said. 'I was up in Sandra's room and someone shot at me. Twice.'

'And didn't hit you even once?' Mr Syme asked as he gently disengaged himself.

'No, I think my screaming put him off. But tell me something, darling – ' She crossed to the front door and closed it. 'As you were walking along the avenue, did you see this man ahead of you?'

'Yes, as a matter of fact, I did,' Mr Syme replied. 'And I saw him turn in at the gate.'

'So it really isn't likely he was the man who shot at me.'

'If you'll tell me just what happened,' Mr Syme said, 'I'll tell you if I think it could have been. But I saw him get off the bus and start walking along the Avenue, getting farther and farther ahead of me, because he walks a good deal faster than I do, but unless this shooting happened literally a second or two before I appeared on the scene, I don't see how he could have been guilty of it.'

Martha turned to Derek Coombes. 'I'm sorry then. I didn't give you a very nice reception.'

'No hard feelings,' he answered, giving her his wide, rather frightening smile again. 'After all, you can't be too careful, the things that happen nowadays. But I'd like to know more about what happened. You said something about someone shooting at Sandra. If anyone's doing that, they've me to reckon with.'

'It was just an idea,' Martha said. 'I may have been wrong. But come upstairs. I'll show you.'

She led the way up and Mr Syme and Derek Coombes followed her.

From the doorway of Sandra's room she showed them the shattered mirror and the chipped plaster of the cornice.

After studying the scene for a moment, Mr Syme said, 'Suppose you show us just where you were when it happened, Martha.'

She went to the bed and stooped over it.

'Just about here. And I happened to look in the mirror and I saw the door open a little way and I had a glimpse of someone outside and I saw a hand come up with a gun in it. And I'm not quite sure what happened then, but I know I threw myself down on the floor and hurt my shoulder and started screaming. Which reminds me, I want some aspirins.'

'Wait a minute,' Mr Syme said. 'You haven't told us just when he fired the two shots.'

'When I started screaming,' she answered.

He looked thoughtful. 'You're sure of what you're saying, are you? You started screaming, then he fired the shots.'

'Yes,' she said.

'Then he went away.'

'Yes. And you do realize, don't you, that if neither you nor Mr Coombes saw him come out of the gate, he may still be in the house or garden?'

'We'll look into that presently,' Mr Syme said. 'Now tell me, did you stop screaming when he fired those shots at you, or did you go on?'

'Oh, I went on. Naturally. I screamed louder than ever.'

'Yet he didn't come back.'

'No. And that's why I had the idea that perhaps he'd really come here to shoot Sandra. I think he may have shot at me more or less automatically before he'd realized he'd got the wrong person. And that would explain why the shots went so wild, wouldn't it? He couldn't stop himself shooting, but he did manage to jerk the pistol up so that he didn't hit me.'

'It's a tenable theory.' Mr Syme turned to the young man who was standing beside him, frowning. 'You are Mr Coombes? Mrs Crayle, in her usual fashion, has forgotten to introduce us.'

'That's right – Derek Coombes,' the young man answered.

'My name is Syme – Edward Syme. Now, Mr Coombes, can you tell me how many people you know who might want to shoot Miss Aspinall?'

'No one!' Derek shouted. 'Asking me how many . . . The bloody nerve! What d'you think she is? She's a nice girl. Not the kind to get mixed up with the kind who carry guns. Not the kind to have enemies, or – or anything. I don't know what this character was at, but you're all wrong if you think he was trying to shoot Sandra.'

Mr Syme nodded. 'As it happens, I can see some holes in Mrs Crayle's theory myself. For one thing, Martha, how many people knew that this was Miss Aspinall's room? Yourself, myself, Mrs Hassall, Mr Turner and Mr and Mrs Gravely. Now assuming that you don't suspect me and that

I don't suspect you, and that you agree that Mrs Hassall, in the hands of the police, has an unassailable abili, do you think the person you saw could have been Mr Turner or Mr or Mrs Gravely? And if it could have been any of them, what could that person have had against Miss Aspinall?'

Martha wrinkled her forehead. 'I don't think it could have been Mrs Gravely, because I think it was a man,' she said. 'But it was such a short glimpse, and I was so scared . . . I suppose it *could* have been a woman.'

'Mrs Gravely is an unusually small woman,' Mr Syme said. 'Did this person give you the impression of being unusually small?'

'No – no, I don't think so. But I don't think he was as tall as Don Turner either. Though perhaps if he'd been crouching . . . No, I don't know. The only thing I'm fairly sure of is that he had a nylon stocking over his head and that his clothes were dark and that he'd a black glove on his hand.'

'The nylon stocking would have prevented you seeing if his hair was red, like Mr Turner's, I suppose,' Mr Syme said.

She nodded. 'I certainly didn't notice.'

'Well, whether he didn't know much about guns and couldn't shoot straight,' Mr Syme said, 'or whether it was Miss Aspinall he wanted to kill and not you, or whether he simply wished to intimidate you while he took a quick look round the house to see if there was anything worth picking up, it would seem you've had a lucky escape. Now I propose we telephone the police. And while we're waiting for them, we can take a quick look round the house ourselves. I don't see much point in searching the garden. If he got as far as that before Mr Coombes and I arrived, he'll be well on his way by now. I suppose you've no idea how he got in, Martha?'

'Oh, of course that was my fault,' she said. 'I know I asked the police who searched the place this morning – did I tell you they'd been here, darling? They searched your room, and I do hope they haven't disarranged anything. They seemed very nice, careful men. Well, I asked them to lock the door behind them when they left, and I know they did, because I had to use my key to get in when I got home, but I probably left the door on the latch then, so that Sandra could get in when she got back. So he probably just walked into the house after me.'

'You'll never learn, will you?' Mr Syme said. But he patted Martha's shoulder as he said it, as if he felt that it was not for him to add just then to what she had gone through that evening. 'Now I'll telephone the police, then I'll search the house.'

'Now wait a minute!' Derek Coombes broke in. 'What about Sandra? Where is she? When's she getting home?'

'I don't know,' Martha answered. 'All I can tell you is, she went out this morning to look for a job. But I should think she might be home any time soon, as offices will all be shut by now. But I'm not at all sure she'll be glad to see you. We heard what she said to you on the telephone yesterday and she most distinctly told you you weren't to come here.'

He grinned again. 'She'll be glad all right. She'll be glad when I say what I've got to say to her.'

'Well, I hope you're right, but I'm not sure,' Martha said. 'I think you may have been just a bit slow making up your mind to say it. You may have lost her.'

He shook his head. 'We're all right, she and I. We understand each other.'

They followed Mr Syme downstairs to the telephone.

He spoke to someone at the police station, was assured, so he told Martha and Derek, that a police car would be round in a few minutes, then he set off to search the house. Beginning in the kitchen he immediately gave a call.

'Come here! This is how he got in.'

From the doorway Martha saw that one of the panes of glass in the window over the sink had been broken. Whoever had come in had only to put his hand through the hole, release the latch and push the window open, then climb over the sink. There were one or two muddy foot-marks on the linoleum between the sink and the door. They seemed to her to be the marks of rather large feet.

'So he got into the house while it was empty,' Mr Syme said, 'and hid till you arrived, Martha. I imagine you didn't come in here when you got home. You could hardly have failed to notice that.'

'No, I went straight up to my room,' she said.

'A pity. If you'd seen that, you could have telephoned the police immediately, and they might have trapped him in the house.'

'And found my body with a few bullets in it if he heard me at the telephone, even if I wasn't the person he'd come after.'

The doorbell rang.

'There they are,' she said, and went quickly to open the door.

But it was not the police she found on the doorstep. It was Sandra. She embraced Martha as if they were the oldest of friends who had not met for months.

'Isn't it marvellous?' she exclaimed excitedly, coming bouncing into the hall, her mane of black hair swinging about her shoulders. 'I've got a marvellous job. It's just what I was looking for, because I can take work home and do it right up to the time the baby comes. It's typing for a secretarial agency. You see, that means I don't have to worry at all about trying to look elegant in somebody's office when I'm getting enormous. I just collect the work from the office in the morning and get ahead with it com-fortably at home – ' She paused, seeing Derek come out of the kitchen. Her vivid features froze. 'What are *you* doing here?' she demanded.

'I just thought – ' he began.

She interrupted, 'I told you not to come here, didn't I? I

told you I'd had enough of you. I only phoned you at all so you shouldn't worry about me. You had your chance and you missed it and now everything's over between us. Mrs Crayle, don't let him stay here. He's no good. He'll only make trouble.'

'I think he'd better stay for the moment,' Mr Syme said. 'We're expecting the police and they might be put out if Mr Coombes had left before they'd had a chance to question him.'

Sandra looked quickly from one face to the other. 'The police? What's happened? Is it about that Hassall girl? Have they found out something? But why should they want to question Derek?'

'There's just been a shooting here, love,' Derek answered. 'And I arrived on the spot just after it happened. I didn't see anything, I didn't hear anything, but here I was on the doorstep only a minute or two later. So I'll have to say my piece to the coppers, stands to reason. Not to worry, though, except that it may have been you the chap thought he was shooting at.'

'Shooting at – *me*?' Her face went blank with incredulity. Then suddenly it blazed with anger. 'Don't try that sort of joke on me, Derek! It's a joke, isn't it? That's all it is. And a damned silly one.' She looked at Mr Syme. 'It isn't true, is it?'

Martha answered, 'Actually someone shot at me. But I was in your room, making your bed, and I screamed so hard he must have known he hadn't killed me, yet he didn't come back and finish me off. So we've been wondering if he'd realized by then I wasn't the person he was after and he'd really been looking for you.'

'No!' Sandra screamed, and her plump face with its ruddy cheeks blazed with rage. 'Nobody's looking for me. Nobody wants to kill me. Why should they? What have I done to anybody? Unless it's him – ' she turned ferociously on Derek again. 'Have you been playing some damnfool trick to frighten me?'

'As it happens,' Mr Syme said, 'I saw Mr Coombes walking along the Avenue some yards ahead of me at the very
time when the shooting was taking place. So I think we can
say for certain that he had nothing to do with it.'

'But what about you, love?' Derek asked with a rather
unpleasant smile. 'I wonder where you were when this
someone-or-other was taking pot-shots at Mrs Crayle. The
police are going to ask you.'

The look of anger had not faded from Sandra's face. Surprisingly violent anger, Martha thought, considering the
circumstances, unless the girl was fairly sure that she had
been the gunman's target.

'Will the police really want to know a thing like that?' she
asked. 'Well, I don't know how long ago it happened, but I
was in the office of Rutley and Rogers – they're the people
who've given me my job – until around five o'clock, and
then I was walking home when I found myself passing the
Compton, and I felt a kind of curiosity – morbid, I suppose
– but I went in and had a drink in the bar and had a look
round. And I met Mr and Mrs Gravely and we chatted for
a little, then I walked on here.'

'Which gives the Gravelys an alibi as well as you,' Mr
Syme said.

'But who was it? Who wants to shoot me?' Sandra's
voice was rising shrilly when the doorbell rang again.

This time it was the police. Mr Ditteridge himself was on
the doorstep. Tall, stooping, unperturbed, he came in, followed by a sergeant, while a constable waited in a car at
the gate. After Mr Ditteridge had asked a few questions,
Martha took him upstairs and showed him Sandra's room,
the broken mirror and the spot in the plaster cornice where
she thought that the second bullet had embedded itself.

He made the inevitable comment that the man had not
been much of a marksman. Martha showed him where she
had thrown herself down on the floor, told him how she

had gone on screaming even after the intruder had left the room, but how he had not come back, and offered her theory that he had come to shoot Sandra and had not returned because by then he had recognized his mistake.

Mr Ditteridge nodded thoughtfully, stroked his craggy jaw and muttered that that was not impossible.

'I'll have to talk to the girl,' he said. 'Was that her downstairs? As it happens, there's something else I want to ask her.'

He and Martha went downstairs again.

She showed him the broken pane in the kitchen window and he nodded again and said that that was undoubtedly how the intruder had got into the house and that he could have been waiting inside for Sandra, or for Martha, as the case might be, for some hours. Then he sent the sergeant upstairs to recover the bullets and called to the constable in the car to make a search of the garden. Martha saw the bright beam of his torch wavering about amongst her untidy shrubs and borders as she went to the bay window in the sitting-room, in which Mr Ditteridge was now confronting Sandra and Derek, and drew the heavy red curtains.

Sandra and Derek were sitting close together, hand in hand, on one of the velvet-covered sofas, as if any animosity between them had been quelled by finding themselves face to face with the law.

Sandra greeted Martha eagerly as she came in, as if she felt sure that she was an ally.

'Derek and I thought we'd go out for dinner as soon as Mr Ditteridge has finished with us,' she said. 'Then we shan't be any bother to you.'

'That's just as you like,' Martha said. 'There's plenty of cold chicken, if you'd like to stay.'

Mr Syme, from behind Mr Ditteridge, started making faces at her. She knew that he did not want her to press Sandra and Derek to stay. He would far sooner have a quiet evening alone with her.

However, Sandra said, 'No, we'll go out. You'll be wanting a bit of a rest after all this fuss. We'll get out of your way as soon as we can. I don't suppose Mr Ditteridge is going to keep us long. There's really nothing we can tell him.'

'Yes, well, now let's go into that,' Mr Ditteridge said, his light brown eyes considering one young face, then the other. 'The first question I must ask you, Miss Aspinall, is, of course, can you think of anyone who might have any reason to shoot you?'

'No,' Sandra and Derek replied together.

'Just Miss Aspinall, if you don't mind, Mr Coombes,' the Superintendent said. 'I'll come to you in a moment. Now, Miss Aspinall, I believe you were sent to Mrs Crayle's house by Miss Mason, Secretary of the National Guild for the Welfare of Unmarried Mothers.'

'That's right,' Sandra said. 'That's to say, Mrs Crayle came into the office when I was there, and Miss Mason asked her if she would take me in for a few days, and Mrs Crayle said yes, and she brought me home with her later.'

'And you met Mrs Hassall that evening?'

'Yes.'

'Had you ever met her before?'

'No, never.'

'Had you ever met Lawrence Hassall?'

'No. Look, what *is* this?' Sandra's voice became shrill. 'I'd never ever heard of either of them. And if I'd known what sort of thing I'd be getting myself into here, I'd never ever have come. Not meaning any ingratitude to you, Mrs Crayle. I know none of this is *your* fault.'

'Quite so,' Mr Ditteridge said. 'But even if you never met either of the Hassalls, Miss Aspinall, there's a question connected with them I want to ask you. You said you met Mrs Crayle in the office and that she brought you home with her later. That means, doesn't it, that you waited there in the office for quite a time?'

Sandra frowned at him suspiciously, as if she were not sure where this line of questioning might lead.

'I suppose so,' she muttered rather sullenly.

'How did you pass the time while you were waiting?'

'I don't know. I looked at some magazines.'

'In the outer office?'

'Yes, Mrs Crayle's office. Miss Mason was working in hers.'

'Did you get up and move about while you were there?'

'I may have.'

'Did you go to the window?'

'I don't remember.'

'Now think, Miss Aspinall.' Mr Ditteridge sounded sterner than before. 'Did you get up and look out of the window?'

'The window!' Sandra exclaimed, her face brightening, as if she had only just understood what he was asking her. 'You mean did I look out at the Compton and did I see anything?'

'Yes, that's the question I was about to ask you,' Mr Ditteridge admitted.

'Then the murder happened in one of those rooms facing the office.'

He nodded. 'Yes, in a room you could have seen from it. And what I want to ask you is whether, when you were standing at the window, you saw anything at any of the windows across the street that caught your attention. Any small thing. A light switched on, for instance, or curtains drawn. Anything at all.'

She smiled. 'But I didn't say I went to the window, did I?'

'Well, did you?'

'I may have,' she repeated. 'I really couldn't say.'

'She did,' Martha said. 'I remember it distinctly.'

Mr Syme, who had been standing behind Mr Ditteridge, gently rocking backwards and forwards on his heels, gave a a slight cough.

'Mr Ditteridge,' he said, 'since you're interested in this young lady, perhaps I should give you a piece of information concerning her which I happened on today by chance. I've been working for a number of years on a History of Medieval Helsington, one of those works, as I know quite well, which will probably never be of the slightest interest to anyone but myself, and which no sane publisher will ever dream of publishing. However, it passes the time for me in what I consider a reasonably constructive fashion. Usually I spend the day in the Helsington Public Library, an excellent one, incidentally. The town should be proud of it. But occasionally I make trips into the country, working on the archives of some of the old houses in the district, or on the parish registers of some of the older churches. And this afternoon I was at St Mary's in Hemlow and there I happened to meet Mr Gorton, the curate – Yes, Miss Aspinall?'

For Sandra had given a queer little gasp. But when Mr Syme looked at her she only shook her head, fiercely pressing her plump red lips together.

'You see, Mr Ditteridge,' Mr Syme continued, 'when Miss Aspinall presented herself to Miss Mason as a candidate for assistance, she gave Mr Gorton of Hemlow as a reference. So naturally I mentioned her to him, and he assured me with regret that he had never heard of her, or of any Aspinalls either, and when I described her appearance to him, he told me he was certain that he had never met her in his life.'

CHAPTER IX

SANDRA'S ROUND CHEEKS puckered as if she were about to cry. She looked frantically at all the faces round her, searching for sympathy. But even Derek Coombes looked disapproving.

'You bloody little fool,' he said. 'Whatever made you tell a yarn like that?'

'Because I didn't know what to do,' she wailed. 'I didn't know where to go. I wasn't going to stay with you after the things you said, and they'd kicked me out of my home long ago and said they were finished with me. Then I remembered the Unmarried Mothers here. A friend told me about them, and about Miss Mason and how she'd helped, but how she'd want a reference and ask all kinds of questions about me. So I thought of Mr Gorton. He isn't telling the truth about never having met me. He just didn't want to let on. I met him on a holiday in France. It was on a bus tour, and he was there with a parson friend of his and we had a lot of fun. Of course I knew Miss Mason would soon find out I'd no right to use his name like that, but I thought perhaps by then she'd think it was a good idea to give me a helping hand anyway. I wasn't going to need it for long, it was just till I got a job and had a little money and could manage on my own. And then of course it turned out she was feeling so ill she didn't do anything about taking up the reference straight away. Anyway, I don't see what difference it makes. I do know Mr Gorton, even if he doesn't remember me, and I could tell you a few things about him that would make his parishioners sit up. Things he'd just as soon I didn't tell them, I shouldn't wonder.'

'Oh God, d'you want to get yourself into trouble for blackmail?' Derek asked angrily. 'Don't listen to her, Mr

Ditteridge. The silly little fool doesn't know what she's saying.'

'Well, would you if you'd just been shot at?' she demanded. 'As a matter of fact, I'm beginning to feel rather queer. Delayed shock, I think. Though I don't really believe it was me they were after at all. I think it was Mrs Crayle all the time and they didn't come back when she screamed because something frightened them off.'

'That's perfectly possible,' Mr Ditteridge said. 'But that would seem to tie Mrs Crayle in with the shooting at the Compton, and that seems unlikely.'

Sandra looked wildly round her again. 'You mean you think *I'm* tied in with that shooting? You believe – oh yes, I know you believe it – it was me that man came after here. And for some reason you think that ties me in with the shooting in the Compton. Why? I don't understand. What have the two things got to do with each other?'

'I'm not at all sure myself,' Mr Ditteridge said. 'But we've never made a habit of shooting one another in Helsington. We massacre one another with motor cars. We have an occasional woman battered to death by a drunken husband. We have cases of rape and strangling and sometimes a whole family of young children destroyed with an axe by a parent who's been driven berserk by the pace of modern living. But shooting's a bit on the sophisticated side for us, and to have two cases of it within twenty-four hours somehow suggests to my simple mind they may be connected. But we'll wait and see. Perhaps those bullets will tell us something.'

He went out into the hall and waited for the sergeant to come downstairs with the bullets.

When they had gone, Derek and Sandra repeated that they were going out and would get something to eat in the town.

'Very kind of you to say we can stay for supper, Mrs Crayle,' Derek said, 'but I think Sandra and I have got to have a talk. I've a feeling there are a good many things we've got to get straight between us. I'll bring her back presently.'

'I don't think we've anything to talk about,' Sandra said. 'I told you I've finished with you, and I don't go in for changing my mind.'

'Not even if I've changed mine?' he asked.

'I don't believe you have,' she said. 'You're only trying to get round me.'

'Well, anyway, come out and have some fish and chips and talk it all over,' he said. 'Is that too much to ask?'

She made a face, but with a shrug of her shoulders agreed to go with him.

As soon as Martha and Mr Syme had the house to themselves, he said predictably, 'A drink! I've seldom felt a more urgent desire for one. But I'm forgetting – how are you feeling, Martha my dear? That experience upstairs must have been extremely upsetting.'

'It's just my shoulder,' Martha answered, rubbing it. 'Be a love and get me the aspirins.'

'Of course. In the bathroom cabinet, aren't they? You just sit down in the kitchen and I'll get them for you with a nice gin and tonic. And if you'll tell me what to do about the cooking, you can put your feet up and have a rest.'

Martha was touched. Mr Syme very seldom offered to help with the cooking. Luckily, perhaps. When he did help, the results were somewhat astonishing.

As he pounded up the stairs to fetch the aspirins she went into the kitchen, settled herself on the sofa, put her feet up and arranged a cushion under her head. When he returned she was absent-mindedly rubbing her shoulder. A slight draught came in from the broken window over the sink, but she had drawn the yellow curtains across it.

He went to the sink, filled a glass of water and brought it to her, together with the aspirins.

She swallowed them and returned the glass to him. 'Of

course, you did it on purpose,' she said.

'Did what?' he asked.

'Went to see Mr Gorton in Hemlow.'

'Well, suppose I did.'

'What I don't understand is why you had to pretend you met him by chance,' she said. 'Why are you never straightforward?'

'No one knows better than you do that I'm normally a very straightforward person,' he said. 'But it seemed to me I'd no right to prejudice the mind of the Superintendent by telling him too much about my own suspicions. That Mr Gorton doesn't know Miss Aspinall, or at least can't remember ever having met her, happens to be a fact. I had no hesitation in telling Mr Ditteridge of it. But my reasons for seeking out Mr Gorton were on the nebulous side, so I thought it was wisest and fairest to everyone concerned to keep them to myself.'

'I know you've been suspicious of Sandra ever since she got here,' Martha said, 'but I don't understand why.'

'But you put those suspicions into my head yourself,' he said, busy pouring out drinks for both of them. 'You pointed out that Miss Aspinall had gone out of her way to tell her boy-friend on the telephone that Mrs Hassall was staying here, and that that could have meant that young Mr Coombes was the individual who telephoned the police to tell them where to find Mrs Hassall. But that implied some connection between the Hassalls and Miss Aspinall and Coombes. So it seemed to me only common sense to check up that very convenient reference of Miss Aspinall's as soon as possible. I felt that you were being sucked helplessly into what might be very deep water and that it was my duty to look after your interests. Not that I got as far as dreaming that someone was going to take a shot at you. If I'd thought of such a thing, I should never have left you alone.'

A vision of Mr Syme in the character of bodyguard, trailing her all over Helsington, perhaps with a revolver on his hip, made Martha giggle.

'But didn't you believe it was Don Turner who telephoned the police about where to find Amanda?' she said.
'And of course it just could have been Don who shot at me
this afternoon. As I said, if he'd been crouching, I couldn't
have judged his height. Thank you, darling . . .' She took
the glass of gin and tonic that Mr Syme had just brought to
her. 'You're looking after me so nicely. In a minute I'll get
up and cook those chops that have lingered in the fridge for
the last few days. The chicken can keep till tomorrow. And
there are some potatoes over from yesterday which I can
fry up, and I'll open a tin of mushrooms and fry some
tomatoes.'

'And what about a bottle of wine?' Mr Syme said.
'Wouldn't that be a good idea?'

'If you feel like it. But are we celebrating something?'

'Just having the house to ourselves, after all the turmoil
you brought into it. You know, Martha, I'm sure you don't
realize how much it means to me just having the place
quietly to ourselves.'

'Yes, well, I like it too,' she admitted.

'I sometimes think you don't. I sometimes think I must
bore you in a terrible way.'

'I'm hardly ever bored, darling. It isn't my nature.'

She did not notice the slightly wry expression that crossed
his face at this not very carefully considered reply.

'Wasn't it boredom that made you get mixed up with
those wretched Unmarried Mothers and so get us involved
in all this?' he asked.

She sipped her drink. 'D'you know what it was that really
got us involved in it all? It was Olive's flu. If Olive hadn't
had flu, I should never have had the chance of asking
Amanda home. Olive wouldn't have allowed it without
finding out a lot about her first. So we should never have
had the police round, looking for her. And next day, if
Olive hadn't still been feeling ill, she'd never have let San-

dra get away with that reference from Mr Gorton. She'd have checked it at once and found it was a fake, and she'd never have planted her on me. So I shouldn't have been shot at this evening. I can't explain quite what I mean, but I've a sort of feeling that Olive's flu may have been an accident that's upset quite a lot of people's planning.'

Mr Syme nodded thoughtfully over his drink. 'Yes, it does look as if there was a good deal of planning in this case that has somehow gone wrong. Hassall's murder, the way Mrs Hassall was manoeuvred on to the right spot at the right time, Turner's presence, which still isn't explained, even the presence of Mr and Mrs Gravely . . . No, I'm responsible for that. I brought them down here. However, it's a fact that a number of people not without reason to desire the death of Hassall were on the spot when it happened. And only Turner has the semblance of an alibi. Yes, that looks like planning. And as Miss Aspinall and Mr Coombes are on the spot too, one's suspicions turn naturally to them. However, Miss Aspinall spent the relevant time with Miss Mason, and so is not under suspicion. But that leaves the field clear for Coombes. Coombes, a not very attractive young man, whom I can easily envisage partnering Hassall in some of his criminal enterprises and then shooting him because of some disagreement that had arisen between them. My dear, I think we've got there. Our murderer is Mr Coombes.'

'But you've given him an alibi yourself for those shots at me – or Sandra, whichever of us they were meant for,' Martha said. 'You said he was walking along just in front of you.'

'Which probably means there's another member of the gang in the neighbourhood whom we haven't uncovered. On the other hand . . .'

'Yes?' Martha said as he paused.

'Nothing. Just an idea. A fleeting thought. Now I'll open that bottle of wine.'

He went out to the old scullery which opened out of the kitchen and was used by Martha as cellar and general store.

'That idea of mine,' he said, returning, 'concerns those bullets the police have taken away with them. They may have something quite interesting to tell us.'

'What d'you mean?' Martha began to get up to go to the refrigerator to take out the chops.

'Stay where you are,' Mr Syme said. 'I told you, I'll cook the supper. But those bullets – if they should be the same, you see, as the ones that came out of the gun that killed Hassall ... They can tell that kind of thing quite easily, you know.'

'Yes, I know. But that would mean Amanda couldn't have killed him, wouldn't it, because she couldn't have shot at me? And it would mean I've been right about her all along and she's just a very nice girl who happens to have had an awful lot of bad luck?'

'Not necessarily. Not for certain.'

Mr Syme lit the gas, went to a cupboard for the frying pan and got busy cooking their supper.

The wine was a not very good Burgundy, but it was warming and calming to the nerves. They did not talk much over their meal. Mr Syme had retreated into what, to judge by his frown and his glazed eyes, was a state of deep concentration, and Martha into a mindless sort of fatigue, which, as she seldom suffered from it, she supposed was probably the after-effect of being shot at. She was longing to go to bed and read a little more of her thriller.

Only a very little more of it, she thought, would put her to sleep. And in her sleep she could count on her dreams, eccentric and ridiculous as they often were, so that she sometimes actually awoke laughing, having nothing to do with murder.

But she and Mr Syme had only just finished the washing-up when the doorbell rang.

She was going to answer it when he thrust himself in her way.

'No,' he said.

'But, darling – '

'No.' He was firm. 'Stand back. You've been shot at once already today and we don't know who's outside. I will open the door.'

Mr Syme in the role of champion and protector fascinated Martha. She had never had cause ever to imagine him in it before. Rather awed, she stood back and watched him as he advanced to the door.

She had to hand it to him, he did not even hesitate before opening it. It reminded her suddenly of the fact that his war record was a distinguished one. He had acquired quite a collection of medals in different parts of the world.

Outside, looking very small, diffident and apologetic, were the Gravelys.

Mrs Gravely spoke for them. 'I do hope you'll forgive us for troubling you at this hour, Mr Syme, but it would be such a comfort if we could come in and talk to you and Mrs Crayle for a little. But please tell us quite honestly if it's inconvenient. We really only came out for a breath of air.'

Martha emerged from behind Mr Syme.

'Yes, do come in,' she said, regretfully abandoning the idea of early bed and the thriller. 'You'd like some coffee, I expect.'

'No, no – please no,' Mrs Gravely said hurriedly. 'We had an excellent meal at the hotel. And we don't want to be any trouble. It's just that it's been such an extraordinary day, and you and Mr Syme have been so kind. We thought if we could have just a little chat with you, it might help us to see things more clearly. We're so confused. Everything we've believed in seems to have been turned upside down.'

She gasped slightly as she allowed herself to be shown into the cold, glittering sitting-room.

'Do you know, the police have been round at our hotel, asking us where we were at half past five,' she went on. 'They told us, Mrs Crayle, that someone had shot at you at that time, and they asked us – *us*, can you believe it? – where we were just then, and could we prove it? That's partly why we wanted to talk to you, of course, to ask you if you could possibly be thinking that either of us could be this lunatic who shot at you. You know, it was such a staggering thing to be asked. I don't think I've ever felt so upset in my life. But you don't believe it, do you?'

'Of course not,' Martha said. 'I'm sure it was routine questioning, the sort of thing they have to do.'

'I don't see the sense of it myself,' Mr Gravely growled. 'I don't see the sense of anything they've been doing. They arrest my daughter and charge her with murder. They suspect my wife and myself of making a murderous attempt on you, when so far as I can make out, we owe you nothing but gratitude for the help you gave Amanda. They asked us why we went to stay at the Compton at just the time when our son-in-law happened to be staying there too. Was that by chance, they asked, or had we some information that he might be found there? What do they take us for? A family of assassins. The local branch of the Mafia?'

'I suppose it was just by chance that you went to the Compton,' Mr Syme observed. 'The Crown in the High Street is generally reckoned the better hotel.'

'Certainly it was by chance!' Mr Gravely answered, his face reddening with resentment at the question. 'We knew nothing about hotels in Helsington, so when you got in touch with us we looked them up in the AA book, found the Crown was a four-star hotel and attempted to get a room there, but they happened to be full. The Compton, only a three star, seemed to be the next best. We telephoned again and obtained a room. Does that explanation satisfy you?'

'Perfectly, perfectly,' Mr Syme said blandly, unaffected by the other man's flare of anger. 'And I'm sure you were able to satisfy the police as to your whereabouts at five-thirty this afternoon.'

'Mr Syme, we didn't come here to be questioned all over again –'

'Sh, dear, sh!' Mrs Gravely said, laying a hand on her husband's arm. 'After all, we came here, didn't we, just to make sure Mrs Crayle wasn't afraid we could have had anything to do with that awful shooting? And I think Mr Syme's quite right to be concerned for her safety, even if it means suspecting people like us. Yes, Mr Syme, we had just met Miss Aspinall in the lounge of the hotel, where we had finished tea, and we chatted for some minutes. I'm sure the waitress, who brought us our bill, which we signed as we were staying in the hotel, will remember us. So now you're satisfied, aren't you?'

'But surely your daughter hasn't been charged with murder yet,' Martha said.

'Well, no,' Mr Gravely admitted. 'I was going a bit fast there. I was allowing myself to be carried away by my feelings. But she's being held in custody, and in her condition, you know, that's terrible. Anything could happen.'

'Have you heard any more about Don Turner?' Martha asked.

Mrs Gravely's eyes suddenly swam with tears.

'No, and that's all our fault – I'm sure it's all our fault!' she cried. 'We always thought he encouraged her in her delusion that Laurie was alive so that he wouldn't have to marry her. And when he told us he wanted to marry her and it was she who said she'd had enough of marriage to last her a lifetime, we were sure it was all pretence. But now I'm sure it was all true and he was really very good and patient with her.'

'But then why did he run out on her when he did?' Martha persisted.

'It's all our fault, all our fault,' Mrs Gravely answered, sobbing quietly.

'I'm afraid my wife isn't very rational at the moment,'
Mr Gravely said. 'I agree we may have misjudged the
young man to some extent, just as we were mistaken in our
doubts of our daughter's sanity. We must have given her a
great deal of unnecessary pain at the time when she needed
our help most. But I don't see how it can help anyone to
blame ourselves for Don's disappearance. Our intuitions
about him were basically quite correct. He's unstable, dis-
loyal and unreliable. I'm very glad Amanda's not married
to him.'

His wife shook her head. 'We're too conventional and
prejudiced, you and I, dear. We don't understand how
young people are today. If we'd welcomed Don into the
family, if we'd accepted him as Amanda wanted us to, she'd
never have turned away from us and then said all those
awful bitter things she did to us this morning. And she and
Don would have had an altogether better, more responsible
relationship, and he'd have stood by her when she needed
him.'

'Well, I don't know, perhaps you're right,' Mr Gravely
said, his bluster dropping from him and his heavy face sagging into lines of weariness and depression. 'Now we've kept
Mrs Crayle and Mr Syme long enough. I'm very sorry our
daughter has brought you all this trouble, Mrs Crayle. But
you know, I don't really believe for a moment it's her fault.
Amanda did not kill Laurie Hassall. It was his criminal
associates who did that. Criminal associates! D'you know,
I still find it almost impossible to believe there could be anything criminal about the boy we remember. He'd been to a
good school, he'd a degree, and he'd such excellent manners.
But for all I know, the standard of manners in prisons is
higher than one would suppose.' He gave an apologetic
smile for his small joke, the first smile that Martha had
seen on his face. 'Now we must thank you and say good
night.'

As soon as they had gone, Martha began to think once

more of going to bed. But first, she decided, she would have a hot bath. Going round the house, locking doors, she realized that with the broken window in the kitchen this was only a ritual action. Anyone who wanted to could get in. But perhaps lightning would not strike twice in the same place. She went up to her bedroom, shed her clothes, put on her dressing-gown, trailed along to the bathroom and turned on both taps. She was lying peacefully relaxed in the hot water when she realized that she had locked Sandra out.

It was an abominable nuisance. Martha did not feel at all like going downstairs again to wait until Sandra came in, at God knew what hour. But Mr Syme had also forgotten her and had gone to his room, and it was unlikely that Sandra would realize that she could easily enter the house by climbing over the kitchen sink.

Reluctantly, Martha recognized that she would have to go downstairs. But she did not hurry her bath. When she had luxuriated in it for as long as she felt inclined, she got out, dried herself, put on her nightdress and dressing-gown, fetched her book from her bedroom and went down to the sitting-room. She had been sitting there only a quarter of an hour when the telephone rang.

It was her elder son, Martin. He was ringing up from the furnished flat in Manchester, where he lived. He said that he had read a small paragraph in his evening newspaper about the murder in Helsington, which mentioned that the woman who was helping the police with their inquiries had been traced to an address in Blaydon Avenue.

'I thought that might be our house, Mother,' he said.

'I don't see why you should think that,' Martha said. 'It seems to me an extraordinary conclusion to jump to.'

'All the same, it *is* our house, isn't it?'

'Well yes. But why you should think so . . .'

'What's been happening, Mother? What trouble have you been getting yourself into?'

'I'm not in any trouble at all. It's the poor girl who's in

trouble. And I'm sure she never did the murder. The more I think about it, the more confidence I have in her absolute innocence.'

'I'm sure you have. And even when she confesses, you'll say it wasn't her fault, that there are excuses for what she did.'

'I don't see why she should confess to a thing she hasn't done. I don't understand you, Martin.'

'Well, never mind. The question is, would you like me to come down and stand by, just in case.'

'In case of what?'

'In case the police bother you, of course, or the Press. It's the weekend, I could easily manage it.'

'It's very, very sweet of you, Martin,' Martha said, 'but no, don't think of it. The only policeman I've seen anything of has been that nice Mr Ditteridge, the one we got to know over that case of arson. He and I get on very well.'

'Mother, I think you're hiding something from me,' Martin said. 'What is it?'

Martin was a shrewd man and understood her, Martha sometimes felt, far better than Jonathan, even though Jonathan, she did not know why, had rather more of her affection. Perhaps it was something to do with her relationship with their two fathers. But at least, she was sure, she had never let either of the boys sense it. Her behaviour to both of them had always been exactly the same. And at the moment she had no intention of letting either of them know that someone had been shooting at her.

'Not at all, dear,' she said. 'And you know Mr Syme's quite capable of dealing with the Press, though they haven't got round to us so far. I don't think this is a sufficiently dramatic murder to interest them, murders happening at the rate they do nowadays.'

'But I'll gladly come if I can help.'

'Thank you, Martin, I do appreciate it. But I'm sure it's

all over as far as I'm concerned. By the way, I had a nice
call from Jonathan yesterday. He and Tilda are spending
the winter in Rome. He sounded wonderfully happy. Martin, I do wish you'd marry. I don't want you turning into
another poor old Mr Syme.'

'Mother, I didn't ring up to discuss my marital problems.
I rang up to ask if I could help you with this murder you've
got involved in.'

'I know, darling, and I do thank you. It was a nice
thought. But really there's nothing you can do. I'd far
sooner you came when everything's normal and we can
have a nice time to ourselves.'

'So things *aren't* normal.'

'Not exactly, no, I must admit that. But truly there's
nothing I can't cope with by myself.'

'If there's any way I can help, will you let me know?'

'Oh, I will, I will. And thank you so much for ringing,
sweetie. Good night.'

As she put the telephone down, Martha gave a sigh. She
did not understand why she never allowed her sons to help
her. It was as if she felt that if she made any demands on
them, she would lose their love. And that was almost certainly unjust to them. But each reminded her so clearly of
his father, and their fathers' love had been so easy to lose,
and for reasons that she had never been able to understand.
There had been Martin's father, who had seemed to her a
sturdy, sensible man, just the kind of man on whom a girl
who was really very shy and not at all sure of herself would
always be able to rely, and he had turned against her because, he had said, she was domineering and bullying. And
there had been Jonathan's father, fragile, amusing, gently,
mildly crazy, and he had left her because, so he had said,
she gave in to him so completely in everything that it
brought out the beast in him and he did not like becoming
acquainted with the beast.

She realized, of course, that what both had said might have had no relation to the truth. They might really have left her because she was not very beautiful, or according to the standards set by their daydreams, not very good in bed. The fear that that might have been the trouble had led her for a time after Jonathan's father had left her, and after she had recovered from an abortive suicide-attempt that she had made then, swallowing a large number, though luckily not enough, of barbiturate capsules, to sleep with almost any man who seemed to want it of her. It had been a curious phase of her life. She had never really regretted it. Undoubtedly it had taught her a great deal about herself. But all of a sudden she had had the feeling of standing on some brink, beyond which was darkness. Only one step forward, she had felt, would send her whirling down into irretrievable disaster.

So she had drawn cautiously back. It had not been easy, and perhaps if it had not been for Aunt Gabrielle, arriving then with her promises and her desperate need for help, Martha would not have had the strength to make the effort to make a serious change in her way of living. But her will was surprisingly strong, once her mind was made up, and in the end she had found a chaste life surprisingly peaceful. At least it saved you from a great deal of grief and pain that you might have suffered otherwise . . .

The doorbell rang.

She went straight to answer it, but just as she was about to open the door, she remembered Mr Syme's caution earlier in the evening, and lifting the lid of the letter-box, called through it, 'Who's there?'

'It's Sandra, Mrs Crayle,' came the answer in a laughing, excited voice. 'And Derek – only of course Derek isn't staying. But I'd like you to meet him just for a minute, because – isn't it marvellous? – we've decided to get married and we'd like you to wish us luck.'

From the way that Martha's face brightened as she flung

the door open, it would have been natural to imagine that her own experience of marriage had been the happiest in the world.

'But that's wonderful!' she exclaimed as Sandra's arms went round her neck and she found herself being warmly kissed on both cheeks. 'So you won't be an Unmarried Mother, and we won't hear any more nonsense about abortions, and – yes, let me think – if it comes to the point, you won't be able to give evidence against each other, will you?'

CHAPTER X

LATER, half-asleep in bed, Martha wondered what had made her say a thing like that. The two apparently very happy young people had laughed loudly at her remark and had said that that of course had been the only reason that had decided them on getting married. But perhaps that laughter had been a little too loud, and hadn't the eyes of both of them, meeting quickly, conveyed some warning to one another?

All imagination, probably. Yet in her drowsy state something preyed on Martha's mind that had struck her earlier in the evening. It was the fact that when Sandra had heard that someone had shot at Martha, only too probably mistaking her for Sandra, she had been extremely angry, but not in the least surprised. Being shot at had been a very astonishing experience for Martha, but not, it seemed, for Sandra. Unless that was imagination too.

Sandra and Derek had taken a great deal of time to say good night to one another on the doorstep. There had been long silences in their whispering to one another, deep sighs and now and then a giggle. Martha, waiting to lock the door, had grown impatient, but had controlled her impulse to interrupt, and at last Derek had gone away, and Sandra had come in, her lipstick smudged and her lips swollen. She had drifted past Martha with dreamy eyes, as if she did not see her, and trailed languidly up the stairs. Martha had fastened the latch after her and gone upstairs to bed.

She overslept next morning and when she came down saw Mr Syme just leaving the house, wearing his overcoat and carrying his briefcase. He paused to tell her that he had got his own breakfast and was on the way to the library.

'Not doing any more detective work today?' she asked.

'Not unless some point of interest that seems to need investigation should occur to me,' he said. 'By the way, Mrs Hassall's back and so is Mr Turner. They're having breakfast. I told them to help themselves, rathen than disturb you, and they seem to be interpreting the suggestion very liberally. You'd think the police have been keeping the young woman short of food from the amount she's eating now.'

'She's eating for two,' Martha said, vaguely remembering that at various stages in her own pregnancies she had been voraciously hungry. 'Well, see you later, darling.'

As Mr Syme left the house, she went to the kitchen.

She found Amanda and Don sitting at the table. There was a packet of cornflakes on it and an opened bottle of milk, plates that looked as if they had had bacon and eggs on them and a pot of coffee. The two of them had reached the toast and honey stage and were talking quietly. They broke off abruptly when Martha appeared and both got to their feet.

'I hope you don't mind my coming back here,' Amanda said. 'I didn't want to go to the Compton, and the police say I've got to stay in Helsington at least till the inquest, and I didn't know where else to go.'

'And helping ourselves to breakfast, I hope that was all right,' Don added. 'Mr Syme let us in and told us to go ahead and not to wake you, as you'd had a rough sort of day yesterday.'

'Well, I was shot at for the first time in my life,' Martha said. 'Perhaps it's a thing that gets easier to stand with practice. Those brave characters on television would never let it upset their digestion, or anything like that, would they?' She took a long look at Don Turner, wondering if he could have been the figure that she had seen on the landing. 'Is that coffee hot?'

'We've just made it,' Don said. 'We were sorry to hear about the shooting. But actually it was because of it that they let Amanda go. The bullets they got out of the room here came from the gun that killed Hassall, and they knew Amanda couldn't have used it to shoot at you.'

'And where have you been all this time?' Martha asked him as she helped herself to coffee.

'A good deal of it at the police station, trying to get them to let me speak to Amanda,' he answered.

'How did you know she was there?'

'They came looking for me at the motel where I'd booked in. She'd given them the address.'

'She seems to have forgiven you for running out on her.' Martha cut a slice of bread and popped it into the toaster. 'Why did you do that, Don?'

He shrugged his shoulders. 'It was just a mood. She seemed to have made up her mind I thought she was guilty – '

'You did,' Amanda broke in. There were hollows under her eyes and her face had the emptiness of extreme weariness. 'You still do, if it comes to that.'

'Anyway, what does it matter now?' he asked. 'We're going to get married, Mrs Crayle, just as soon as we can fix it. The police want both of us to stick around, but they never said anything about not getting married.'

'I think I'll start running this house as a marriage bureau,' Martha said. 'A lonely hearts club. That's two marriages that have got themselves fixed up here during the last twelve hours.' She restrained herself from mentioning the fact that, like Sandra and Derek, Don and Amanda would not have to give evidence against one another. 'I hope you'll be very happy. This is very good coffee, whichever of you made it.'

'Don made it,' Amanda said. 'And thank you very much for your good wishes. Of course, I've wanted to marry Don almost from the first. I admit I was prejudiced against it to begin with, after my experience with Laurie, but now it's different. It helps that Don doesn't think I'm mad any more, he only thinks I'm a murderess.'

He put a hand on her shoulder and shook her gently. 'Why d'you pretend to believe that?' he asked. 'Everyone knows you can't be because you couldn't have shot those bullets at Mrs Crayle. And I was ready to marry you even when I thought you were mad, remember? So stop trying to get at me. I might get tired of it.'

The piece of toast popped up out of the toaster. Martha spread butter and honey on it.

'Why d'you think anyone should want to shoot at me?' she asked. She wondered what these two, who had not heard all the discussion that there had been on the subject, would have to say to that.

'I suppose someone thinks you know something about Hassall's murder,' Don replied. 'You were out in the street, weren't you, about the time it happened? Perhaps someone thinks you saw them going into the Compton.'

'It would have to be someone I know, or my seeing them wouldn't mean anything.'

'Of course.'

'Don't you remember noticing anyone yourself, Don, while you were standing on our steps? You were there for quite a while. Weren't there any people you could describe to the police?'

'There was a certain amount of coming and going,' he answered, 'even up and down your staircase, but no one I noticed particularly. There was one woman who spoke to me about the weather – oh, that was you, wasn't it? That's why I've had the feeling of having seen you before. It's been puzzling me. But really I was only thinking about Amanda.'

'One thing I don't understand is how you knew she was going to be there,' Martha said. 'The Gravelys didn't tell you, did they?'

'No, it was Amanda herself who gave me the information.'

'She said she didn't.'

'I didn't mean to,' Amanda said. 'But when I had that telephone call that told me I'd find Laurie at the Compton in Helsington on Thursday, I wrote it down on the pad beside the telephone. And I did it with a ballpoint pen and later, when I'd left and taken that piece of paper with me, Don managed to read what I'd written on the sheet underneath it and came down here to watch for me.'

'Luckily for you,' Don said.

Amanda raised her eyes and they gave one another a long look.

Puzzled, because that look was not a loving one, though it had a shared, apprehensive understanding in it, Martha poured out more coffee for herself and made a second piece of toast.

Then, while she ate the toast, she started to make out her shopping-list for the weekend. She would go out immediately after breakfast, she thought, in the hope of getting ahead of the Saturday morning queue. But even if you went early the supermarket was generally impossible on a Saturday, and so was the only good greengrocer in the district. She wanted to change her library books too and she ought to go to the local joiner to see if he would come to mend the broken window. So she would be gone for a good while, and probably ought to find out from these two before setting out what plans they had for the day. And there was Sandra, still in bed. Perhaps Martha ought to go upstairs to wake her.

But in the end she decided to let the girl lie, hoping that she would have the sense to get some breakfast for herself when she got up. Don and Amanda told Martha not to worry about them. They were not sure what they were going to do, but anyway would go out. Putting on her coat and taking her handbag and shopping trolley, Martha set out for the shops in the High Street.

She was gone even longer than she expected because she happened to run into a friend in the supermarket who sug-

gested that they should have coffee together. It made a nice
change for Martha, because the friend had heard nothing
about the murder, and anyway was the kind of woman who
thinks that her own children are the only subject worth talking about. She had three and they all had the psychological
problems appropriate to their different ages, and by the
time that she had explained them all and Martha had
reached home, it was twelve o'clock and Don and Amanda
had gone out. Sandra apparently had gone out too, for her
room was empty, as Martha could see through the open
door when she went to her own room to take off her coat.

Sandra's bed was a rumpled mess, as it had been the day
before, and her belongings were strewn about the room,
mostly on the floor. Hesitating in the doorway, Martha had
a certain inclination to go in, to repeat her movements of
yesterday, to see if any memory would come to her of that
figure that she had seen for an instant on the landing, of the
gloved hand rising with the gun in it. She stepped forward.

But as soon as she took that step she felt her skin grow
pimply with gooseflesh and a trickle of ice run down her
spine. She stepped back quickly, slammed the door and ran
straight downstairs.

It was utterly absurd, of course. It was just blind, un-
reasoning panic. The last place where the gunman would
ever reappear would be in Sandra's room. And Martha did
not usually allow herself to have attacks of nerves. There
had not been many periods of her life when she had been
able to afford them. Yet the truth was that just then she was
extremely frightened, and of nothing more than a hazy
memory and a glimpse of a shattered mirror, and of the
emptiness of the house and of the feeling that somewhere in
that emptiness ears might be listening, eyes watching for
her.

She tried to steady her breathing. She had never been one
of the women who are scared of spending a night alone in
a house, and this was not even night-time, it was mid-day.

Grabbing the kettle, she filled it, deciding to make herself some more coffee, not the instant kind, but the real thing and good and strong, as Don's had been at breakfast.

Just then she noticed an odd thing. Not that she gave it much thought till later. Don and Amanda had apparently washed up before they had gone out, for there were no egg-stained plates on the table, or bowls that had held corn-flakes, and the coffee-pot had been put away. Yet there were still two cups on the table with coffee dregs in them, besides a jar of instant coffee and a milk bottle. The lid of the coffee jar had not been replaced.

That looked typically like Sandra's work, Martha thought. She must have got up while Martha was out, come down and helped herself.

But two cups had been used. So Sandra had had company.

Derek, of course. Not in itself a surprising thing. After all, Martha could not be absolutely certain that he had not spent the night in the house. Sandra could easily have slipped downstairs and let him in after Martha had gone to bed. And that thought, a little to her own surprise, gave her a twinge of uneasinsss.

To admit the truth, she had not much taken to him. Perhaps it was just prejudice left over from what Sandra had said about his being ready to marry her if she would have an abortion. That had seemed so abominably selfish. And for all that Martha knew, it was still his price for agreeing to the marriage. But since Sandra had been shown to be a liar about certain other things, that story about the abortion might even not have been true. Yet a feeling that there was something hard and unreliable about Derek Coombes lingered in Martha's mind. She was not sure that she cared much for the thought of his coming and going in the house when she was not here.

After all, there had been a murder in Helsington and another attempted one in this very house . . .

No, Martha told herself irritably, that was nerves, all nerves. Derek could not have shot at her. Mr Syme himself had guaranteed that. There was probably nothing wrong with the boy but a bit of youthful irresponsibility. And as Sandra had a good deal of the same quality, they would probably suit each other admirably. Better than Martha had suited either of her husbands. Who was she to cast stones?

Making a cheese sandwich, she settled down to eat it and drink the strong, fresh coffee.

However, as she set out presently for the offices of the National Guild for the Welfare of Unmarried Mothers, she was curiously obsessed with the image of Derek Coombes. The bulging shoulder muscles, the long, rather simian arms, the bullet head that seemed attached to his body without any neck to speak of, the bright eyes under their heavy lids and the puckered, pouting lips, could easily develop, when the softness of youth was gone, into someting loutishly brutal. Martha did not think that she would like to be Sandra if Derek happened to come home drunk.

But perhaps it would not be so good being Derek if Sandra happened to come home drunk. There was a kind of brutality in the girl as well as in the young man which at first Martha had thought of as a kind of healthy toughness, which had rather attracted her, but which now, for some reason, she did not find so appealing. Could Mr Syme be wrong about that alibi, she wondered. Could it have been Derek who had shot at Martha's reflection in the mirror, thinking that he was ridding himself of Sandra?

The strong wind of the day before had dropped, and there was a stillness in the air that promised frost. The blue of the sky was pale and coldly clear. The sun was low already, shining into Martha's eyes as she walked down the narrow street towards the office. As she climbed the stairs to it, she realized that the door was open, because even before she had reached the landing, she could hear excited voices coming from inside.

'*Everything*, I tell you, Olive! Everything I've got!' The voice belonged to Lady Furnas, although it was pitched so much higher than usual that for a moment Martha almost doubted it. 'Except, of course, what I had with me. But I never take much when I travel, and never anything valuable. Oh, I feel such a fool, Olive – that's what I really feel most, a fool!'

Olive Mason replied, 'Bloody for you, anyway. I mean, having someone pawing through your things. That always seems to me one of the most horrible things about a burglary. The invasion of your home. But you're lucky they didn't foul the place up. I believe that often happens.'

Martha pushed the door wider open and went in.

'Oh, Martha!' Althea Furnas exclaimed, swinging round on her perch on the edge of Martha's desk. 'What d'you think's happened? We've been burgled.'

She was an unusually tall and very slender woman of forty, with a long pale face which even a month in the Caribbean had failed to tan, very pale grey eyes and a rather toothy but attractive smile. Her thick straight hair had gone grey early and was swept back from her face into a simple roll. Her lipstick was a very light pink and the tweed of her dress was all in soft tones of pink and grey. Everything about her was in faint, washed-out colours. Yet she gave an impression of restless vitality as well as obstinate will-power. She was the wife of a man much older than herself who had been Governor of one of those new African countries the names of which Martha could never remember, but the wealth of the couple was mostly Althea's. Her grandfather, who had started as a small builder, had bought land in the right place at the right time, and had handed down a considerable fortune to his descendants.

'Your jewellery?' Martha said, taking off her coat. 'It's been stolen?'

'Every scrap,' Althea Furnas answered. 'We've had the

police in all the morning. They've been sneering at that old safe of ours, saying anyone could have broken into it with a tin-opener. But apparently this thief of ours was a bit of an artist. He didn't use explosives or anything crude. He did something clever about listening to the tumblers or something. I don't really understand it. It's a slow way of doing things, the police said, but he obviously knew we were away and knew we'd given the Greens a holiday.' The Greens were the couple who looked after the Furnases. 'So he just took his time, never left a single fingerprint and made a clean sweep.'

'But at least the things were insured, weren't they?' Olive said. She was huddled in her coat, close to the little electric fire, but was looking more herself today, although her voice was still hoarse. 'You'll be able to replace them.'

'You can't really replace the things you care about,' Althea said. 'Some of the things I liked most were actually the least valuable I had, things Douglas and I picked up on an impulse when we were feeling happy and suddenly wanted to celebrate we didn't quite know what. But I tell you, I feel such a *fool*. And Douglas thinks the right way to cheer me up is to tell me that if I'd had any sense I'd have kept all the stuff in the bank. I simply hate the thought of keeping jewellery in a bank. Half the fun of having it is being able to play with it when you want to. And I was just telling Olive, Martha, it seems our thief is probably your murdered man. And your murderer probably stole my jewellery from our thief and is God knows where by now, after arranging for your Amanda Hassall to get arrested. At least, that seems to be how the police have worked it out so far. What a lot I've been missing!'

'I expect the police have told you they've let Amanda loose,' Martha said. 'Someone shot at me yesterday, using the same gun that was used to kill Laurie Hassall. And of course that couldn't have been Amanda. But I can't help feeling it just could have been Sandra or her boy-friend.

Olive, do you know that Mr Gorton of Hemlow has never heard of Sandra? That reference she gave you was a complete phoney.'

Olive gave Martha a puzzled look, popped a lozenge into her mouth and said explosively through a blast of menthol, 'Someone shot at you yesterday – Martha, what are you saying? Why the hell should anyone want to shoot at you?'

Martha told Olive and Althea the story of the shooting and of the suspicion that the intended victim had been Sandra.

'No,' Olive said hoarsely. 'I don't believe it. And I don't believe there's anything wrong with her reference. I know I didn't check up when I should have, I was feeling so lousy, but – no, I don't believe it. She's so obviously genuine. I can always tell.'

'I'm sorry.' Martha knew that Olive's belief in her own ability to size up other people correctly was very precious to her. 'Mr Syme had his doubts about her from the beginning, so he went out to Hemlow to investigate, and Mr Gorton said he'd never heard of her or of the people she said were her parents.'

'Oh God, oh God!' Olive clasped her forehead in both hands. 'It's all my fault then, is it? Leaving you in charge here so that you collected that Hassall girl, and then not checking those references. If it hadn't been for this bloody flu . . . I haven't been up to the job. But who *is* the girl then? Sandra, I mean. How's she got mixed up in all this? Did she do the murder? No, she can't have. She was in this room all that afternoon. But perhaps she gave a signal of some sort from the window to the boy Coombes. I might not have seen that. And the signal would have meant she'd seen Hassall arrive in his room and it was time for Coombes to go up and kill him and take Althea's jewellery. I suppose they weren't satisfied with the cut Hassall was giving them, or something like that. And then Coombes tried to shoot Sandra so that he could keep all Althea's stuff himself and perhaps get rid of the baby and take up with some other girl – no, you said your Mr Syme gave Coombes an alibi for that shooting. Oh Christ, I can't make head or tale of it. I'm not myself, but I do see it's all my fault and I'm ready to resign. Althea, I'll resign this moment if you want me to. Just say the word. I'll type out my letter of resignation here and now.'

Althea gave Olive one of her vague looks and murmured, 'You're getting so excited, Olive. I expect you've a temperature. And of course all these things aren't your fault. The trouble is, you've a much too orderly mind. You're trying to connect everything up together, when the chances are they're just a mess. I don't pretend to understand much of it, and really I don't care about any of it except that my lovely jewellery's gone. There was an aquamarine ring I simply adored, not a quarter as valuable as my rather awful emeralds, but it was my sort of thing, it suited me, I felt really happy when I wore it. And there was an enamelled brooch with pearls and garnets – eighteenth century – oh, I mustn't go on about it. But I don't mind a bit if someone killed that horrid Hassall. Now I'm going home. I expect the place is still infested with police and insurance assessors and reporters. Douglas will be coping with them, of course, so perhaps I can dodge them and just go to bed. That's all I really want to do at the moment. After our night-flight I haven't got used to what time of day it is, and the climate seems perfectly horrible after Barbados. But telephone me, of course, if anything too drastic happens.'

Picking up a rather battered mink jacket which she seemed to consider appropriate to wear to the office, she drifted out.

There was silence for a moment after she had gone, then Olive got up wearily from her chair and crossed to the window. With her shoulders hunched and her hands dug deep into her pockets, she leant her forehead against the glass as if its coldness relieved the burning of her skin. She

looked out woodenly at the dreary front of the Compton
Hotel.

'I don't understand Althea,' she said. 'Imagine worrying
more about that junk of hers than about a murder and you
being shot at – you, for God's sake!'

'I think it's her way of putting a brave face on things,'
Martha answered. 'She's pretending all she cares about is
the jewellery because thinking about all the rest of it is just
a bit too much for her. But she's a very human person
really. She hates this violence as much as you or I do.'

'You really think so?' Olive sounded sceptical. 'But it's
the kind of thing you usually think about people, isn't it?
They're all so human, they're all so good-hearted. I wonder
how you'd act if you came up against a really evil person,
Martha.'

'I'm not sure I believe in really evil people.'

'Then it's time you learnt. They're all around you. And
sooner or later you may have to deal with one. So you might
give the matter some thought.'

'Well, I always find it's easier to trust people than not to,'
Martha said. 'I dare say it's a kind of laziness. I honestly
don't like the sensation of distrust. It's as if something was
crawling over my skin like earwigs. But you aren't suggest-
ing darling Althea's evil.'

Olive gave an abrupt laugh. 'Why not, after all? And
wouldn't it be amusing if she were? Suppose she and
Douglas really got home from the West Indies several days
ago – that postcard she sent me could have been a blind –
and suppose they'd arranged with Hassall to steal the jewellery for the sake of the insurance, then murdered him because he tried to blackmail them about it, and took a pot-
shot at you because they thought you'd recognized one or
other of them in the street . . .' She broke off with a guffaw
which developed into a fit of coughing. 'Forgive my sense
of humour,' she said. 'If that's what it is. Really I'm feeling
so sick at myself for not checking that reference that my

head's going round. Where's the girl now, d'you know? Is she at your house?'

'She wasn't when I left, and she can't get in till I or Mr Syme get in, unless she thinks of climbing in by that broken window. The joiner wouldn't come today, because it's Saturday and he's going to watch football, but he promised he'd come on Monday. Meanwhile anyone can get in.'

'I'd get rid of her as soon as you can,' Olive said. 'I feel bad about having unloaded her on to you.'

'Oh, she's all right,' Martha said. 'I don't really believe she's got anything to do with any of these horrid things. She's a bit untidy, that's all. Never makes her bed and never hangs up any of her clothes. I do find it rather irritating in a guest. In your own home, of course, you've a right to do as you like, but in someone else's you should try to be considerate.'

'I do admire your scale of values,' Olive said. 'I envy you really. You must be much happier than most people. Now I'd better get down to some work or I'll never catch up with the bloody heap of letters that's been piling up.'

She went into her own office while Martha settled down to add another inch or two to her knitting.

She wondered if it was true that she was happier than most people. It had never occurred to her before that she might be. Without having the habit of feeling sorry for herself, she was accustomed to thinking that she had had a generous share of misfortunes, and that though there was nothing to be gained by brooding on them too much or becoming tiresome to other people by continually talking about them, yet she had not had quite the luck in life that seemed to come to a lot of people. But perhaps she was wrong and she had had more luck than she deserved. Wonderful things had happened to her. Aunt Gabrielle, for instance, poor, sweet, old thing. And the two boys, both growing up so loyal and affectionate. And even Mr Syme. Edward darling. His companionship during these last few years had really meant more to her than she had given him credit for. Considering what a highly intelligent man he was, it was astonishing how much time he had for someone like her. Then he was generous, he was thoughtful and reliable, he was tidy . . .

That untidy bedroom of Sandra's was on Martha's mind when she reached her home that evening. As soon as she had been to her own room, taken off her coat and run a comb through her hair, she went straight to Sandra's room to straighten it. She made the bed, hung Sandra's dressing-gown on the peg on the door, picked up the clothes strewn about the floor, then opened the vast wardrobe that took up almost one whole side of the room, a wardrobe which Aunt Gabrielle had insisted on buying because it was of such good quality, and so cheap, but for which there had never been any convenient place in the house. And reaching inside for a hanger on which to drape a blouse that had lain crumpled on the carpet, Martha discovered Sandra.

She was crouched on the floor of the wardrobe, folded into an impossible heap of limbs, which Martha knew, without putting out a hand to touch them, were stiff and cold. The girl's face was hidden under the fall of her thick, dark hair, but the neck was bare and Martha could see a bright orange cord, the belt of the dress that Sandra had worn the day before, deeply embedded in the yellow-grey flesh, knotted tightly round it.

Not someone who was going to become one of life's victims, Mr Syme had said. For once he had been wrong.

CHAPTER XI

MARTHA FLED down the stairs. She flung herself down them so fast that she nearly tripped. Snatching up the telephone, she dialled. She had dialled more than half the numbers before she realized that it was not the police station that she was ringing, but the city library. It had been automatic, in the state of shock that she was in, to try to get in touch with Mr Syme.

She hesitated, her finger poised above the telephone, then she finished dialling the library number. There was no answer. Naturally, since the library closed at five. The place was empty already. A good thing, really, since it meant that Mr Syme must be on his way home. Unless by any chance he had stopped at his club for a drink.

Her finger hovered uncertainly over the dial for a moment, as she wondered whether or not to ring the club. But of course the right thing was to ring the police station immediately.

She dialled and spoke to a sergeant whose voice she was beginning to know. She almost felt that there was an unfriendly abruptness about ringing off without asking how his wife and children were and to ask him if they had made any nice plans for their summer holidays. That had become such a safe subject to raise on almost any occasion. But there was a finality about the way that he told her that a police car would be round in a few minutes which showed that she would not hurt his feelings by ending the conversation. Putting the telephone down, she wandered into the kitchen.

She kept waiting for the squeak of the garden gate that would tell her that Mr Syme had arrived, but she heard only the usual traffic noises of the street. The kitchen felt

unusually cold. The wind must have changed and be blowing in more directly at the broken window than it had
earlier. She looked at the jagged hole which showed her a
patch of dead blackness in the midst of all the shiny reflec-
tions thrown back by the unbroken panes. Her own figure
roamed from one to another of them as she moved restlessly
about the kitchen.

That dead patch began to fill her with a certain dread, as
if something all too alive might appear outside it at any
moment. She began to think of blotting it out in a tempor-
ary sort of way with some cardboard and drawing-pins.
She had some cardboard, she thought, some old dress-boxes,
in the scullery, where most of the litter of the house accumulated. Going out to the scullery, she had just found the
lid of a box which she thought she could cut down con-
veniently to the size of the pane when the telephone rang.

She ran to it as if it must be something of importance,
although she was not expecting any particular call just then.

As soon as she spoke a voice said, 'It's Derek, Mrs Crayle.
Is Sandra there?'

'Well . . .' The question was actually a very complicated
one. You could flounder into metaphysics, if you weren't
careful, trying to answer it. 'Well, no, not exactly,' Martha
said. 'Where are you, Derek?'

'I'm at the railway station. Do you know where Sandra
is?'

'No, I – I can't really tell you much about that.'

'I've been phoning her all day and haven't had any
answer. I even came round to your house in the afternoon
and rang and rang your doorbell, but no one answered.'

'I'm afraid I've been out most of the day myself,' Martha
said. 'That's why you didn't get any answer. But why don't
you come here now?'

'Do you know where she went? She told me she'd stay in
till I rang.'

'Haven't you seen her at all today?'

'No, not since last night. We arranged then we'd meet at the station to catch the five-fifty to London, but I was to telephone her in the morning to see – ' He paused, as if he had almost said something that he had not intended. 'Well, to see if she still wanted to go with me,' he went on. 'Yesterday she said she would, then at the last moment she said her mind wasn't absolutely made up, so would I phone.'

'But didn't you see her this morning, Derek? Didn't you have coffee with her?'

'No.'

'Well, someone did,' Martha said. 'I found the cups and the coffee jar on the kitchen table.'

'It wasn't me, Mrs Crayle. But someone, you say, had coffee . . . Alone with her?'

'I suppose so. Just the two cups had been used.'

'Is Sandra all right then? The way you talk, it sounds kind of funny.' The way he talked himself sounded funny. His voice had risen a semitone. There was sudden panic in it.

'The fact is, Derek, I don't know what to tell you about that,' Martha answered. 'I've a feeling I ought to say nothing. Only it doesn't seem fair. No, I'm afraid Sandra isn't all right at all. A frightful thing's happened – '

'Goodbye, Mrs Crayle. Sorry I can't wait. My train's just coming in. Tell Sandra I'm sorry I couldn't wait, but I'll see her in London. Goodbye now.'

The line went dead. The sound of the terrified voice in Martha's ear was cut off.

Replacing the telephone slowly, she realized that the hand that had been holding it was shaking. Either Derek knew of Sandra's murder and had been trying to find out if it had been discovered yet, or else it was something that he had half-expected, and he had been able to guess, in spite of Martha's evasions, that it had happened. And he wanted no part of it.

The police arrived almost immediately afterwards. First

there were two constables, who took a look in the room that
had been Sandra's, then started talking into the two-way
radios they carried. Superintendent Ditteridge, they told
Martha, would be here in a few minutes.

They were waiting for him in the hall when the gate gave
its familiar squeak and Mr Syme let himself into the house.

Clinging to him before the police could intervene, she
told him of her discovery of Sandra's body, and saw him
nod his head thoughtfully, as if he were telling her that he
could have warned her, if only she had asked for his advice,
that all this was likely to happen. Then he went upstairs to
his rooms to take off his coat and deposit the books that he
was carrying. He came down again just as Superintendent
Ditteridge arrived.

He was taken upstairs by one of the constables, then
almost at once got to work on the telephone, with the result
that a large number of people came to the house, a doctor,
an ambulance, some photographers and some men who
blew a great deal of grey dust about the house, which
Martha realized it would be a detestable job to clean up.
She and Mr Syme were almost ignored for what felt a very
long time, though Mr Ditteridge told them, in the midst
of giving orders to other people, that he wanted to talk to
them.

Because of the draught in the kitchen, they waited for
him in the sitting-room, lighting the gas fire and drawing
the velvet curtains in an effort to take the chronic chill out
of the room.

Sitting close to the fire, shivering partly from cold and
partly from nerves, Martha said, 'Darling, what do you
think about double-glazing?'

'For God's sake!' Mr Syme said wearily, as if he were too
tired to try to follow the workings of her mind.

'Well, this room's always icy, isn't it?' she said. 'We don't
usually notice it because we hardly ever use it. But with all
this coming and going we've been having, bringing people

in here because it didn't seem quite appropriate to take them into the kitchen, I've been realizing what a dead loss the place is. But if we had an off-peak heater in here and double-glazing, we could make it quite nice and cosy.'

Mr Syme gave an austere look round him.

'You'd have to re-furnish it,' he said. 'A good deal of the chill is psychological. Your dear aunt had deplorable taste in furniture. There's nothing that strikes quite such a chill to the bone as shiny velvet on your chairs and sofas.'

'But it's all awfully *good* stuff,' Martha said, 'and I'm sure if we tried to sell it we'd get next to nothing for it.'

'You don't *need* anything for it,' he replied. 'Why can't you get it into your head you are not a poor woman? You could afford to give all this stuff as a gift to the Salvation Army and start again from scratch, choosing the things you really like.'

'Only, d'you know, I don't trust my own taste,' she said. 'It might end up just as bad as it is now.'

'I would help you to the best of my ability,' he said. 'There'd be no hurry. We could explore the local antique shops one at a time – '

'Oh darling, wouldn't that be fun? Shall we really do it?'

'Why not? And I wouldn't disdain the modern either, if it's of adequate quality. I know a young couple who've recently started up in Helsington, designing and making some really excellent things – '

'Edward, Edward, what utter nonsense we're talking!' Martha, who had squatted down on the rug in front of the fire, gave her head a violent shake. 'There's been a murder in this house, don't you remember? And I've such a lot to tell them when they get round to me. And we sit here, talking about furnishing this room!'

'It seems to me a very innocuous subject,' Mr Syme said. 'We've got to talk about something. To sit in a deathly silence would be morbid. But what a time you're having, my poor Martha, finding corpses and being shot at. I used to have a nurse when I was a child who said things always came in threes. And I'm often astonished at how often this turns out to be correct, even when I'm writing it off as pure superstition. So I wonder what your number three is going to be.'

'Haven't we had all three already?' Martha said. 'You've forgotten about the murder in the Compton.'

'No, I hadn't forgotten it. It was just that that didn't seem to have any close connection with you. The other two things have happened in your house.'

Martha gave a little wriggle on the hearthrug. 'I don't much care for the sound of that. Something else is to happen here, is it? Or to me? D'you know, I can't imagine you with a nurse. I bet you gave her hell. What was she like? A Gorgon who trampled on you and left you with a great fear of women, or someone so sweet you've never been able to find anyone to match up with her? And did she dress you in velvet suits and lace collars? You'd have looked gorgeous in velvet and lace.'

'Thank you, but your sense of period is letting you down, I'm afraid,' Mr Syme replied. 'Little Lord Fauntleroy was definitely out by the time I was born. Sailor-suits were the right thing for well-dressed children of my age.'

Martha abruptly began to cry.

'Oh, darling, how sweet you are!' she said through her snuffles. 'You're only trying to keep my mind off that horrible thing that happened upstairs. I don't believe you ever had a nurse. Now be honest. Did you? Didn't your poor mum work her fingers to the bone, looking after you all by herself?'

'No, my mum, as a matter of fact, was a very idle woman. She hated movement. She liked to sit quietly by the window, putting on weight, and doing beautiful embroidery which she gave away to sales for various charities. My father was one of the more successful surgeons here in Helsington

– haven't I told you all this often before? I don't want to bore you.'

'You've hardly ever told me anything about yourself. For all I know, you could have sprung, fully-armed, from Jove's forehead.'

'Really? Then I suppose I didn't think the subject was interesting. We weren't exactly wealthy, you know, just what I think you could call well-to-do. But in those days you didn't have to be wealthy to be able to afford two or three servants and a nurse and a gardener. But unfortunately the nurses never stayed for long, though whether that was because I was a quite intolerable child or because my mother was difficult I really don't know. I remember, however, that in my earliest years I used to give these good women my ardent affection, but that led to so much suffering when they went away that I took to treating them with a sort of contempt, which I suppose they found extremely aggravating.'

'And with which you've gone on treating almost everyone ever since – darling, aren't we getting Freudian?' Martha had relaxed more comfortably on the hearthrug. 'But what a come-down you must have found it, after all that grandeur, coming to live here. I realize, of course, there was an interval, the war and all that, when you may have got used to hardship.'

'My years in this house have been the happiest in my life,' Mr Syme said.

Martha was so moved that she felt an impulse to reach up and kiss him, a thing that she had done only on very special occasions in all the time that she had known him, although she kissed most of her friends, male and female, in an easy, social way and without stopping to think about it. But before the impulse could turn into action the door opened and Mr Ditteridge, followed by one of the other detectives, came in.

'I'd like a talk with you now, Mrs Crayle,' the Superintendent said. He looked tired and abstracted, as if he did not think that she would have much to tell him. 'There are some questions I must ask.'

'Of course.' Martha stood up and sat down again in a chair instead of on the floor, the change of posture helping her to jerk herself from one mood to another. She gestured at chairs for the two men. 'It's her boy-friend who did it, isn't it? It has to be.'

'When there's a murder,' Mr Ditteridge said, 'unless it's a gang killing, it's usually the husband or wife or the boy-friend or girl-friend who turns out to be the one we want. But had you some other reason for saying that?'

'It's just that I think he had coffee with her here this morning,' Martha said. 'Someone did. There were two used cups on the kitchen table. But when Derek telephoned me just a little while ago from the railway station – at least, he said he was at the station, but of course I'm not sure where he really was, but I think I heard railway noises in the background – he said he hadn't seen her since last night and had been trying to get in touch with her all day. But as soon as I told him about her having coffee with someone this morning, he said his train had just come in and he couldn't wait and he rang off. It sounded as if he was running away.'

'How long ago was this?' Mr Ditteridge asked abruptly, with a sudden awakening of interest on his tired face.

'A few minutes before you got here.'

The Superintendent turned on his companion, gave him quick orders to check the trains, then turned back to Martha.

'You didn't see Coombes here this morning yourself then?'

'No.'

'When did you last see the girl?'

'Last night.'

'Not this morning?'

'No.'

'Not at breakfast?'

'No, I didn't give her breakfast. I thought she could get her own when she felt like getting up. When I came down I found Amanda Hassall and Don Turner in the kitchen and they'd got breakfast for themselves. They told me Mr Syme had let them in.'

Mr Syme nodded. 'They arrived just as I was going out. I told them not to disturb you.'

'Well, they were still in the kitchen when I went out to do my shopping,' Martha went on. 'Sandra was still in bed. Or I supposed she was. I didn't look in on her to make sure. Then I was gone for a couple of hours and when I got back I found Don and Amanda had left and had washed up their breakfast things and put everything tidily away, but there were two cups on the kitchen table and a jar of instant coffee and a milk bottle. So I realized Derek must have come in and had coffee with Sandra, and then, as she wasn't about, I thought of course they'd gone out together.'

'What did you do with the cups?'

'I washed them up.'

Mr Ditteridge cracked his knuckles. 'Of course, of course. If only women hadn't this mania for washing up. The amount of evidence that goes down the drain!'

'But I never dreamt of anything being wrong, Mr Ditteridge,' she excused herself.

'Well, what about the milk bottle? What about the jar of coffee?'

'The milk bottle's in the fridge. I put the coffee jar back on the shelf where I always keep it.'

'Will you show me, please?'

She took him out to the kitchen, opened the refrigerator and was going to take out the half-empty milk bottle when he checked her.

'No need to add any more of your fingerprints, Mrs

Crayle. Not that we're likely to find anything useful. There'll be your prints, and the milkman's, and Mrs Hassall's and perhaps Turner's, and perhaps the Aspinall girl's too. She probably did the pouring out. But we aren't likely to find the prints of Coombes or whoever had coffee with her. Now what about the coffee jar?'

Martha showed him where it was kept. He summoned one of his men and had the jar and the bottle wrapped up in plastic and taken out to one of the waiting cars.

Returning to the sitting-room with Martha, Mr Ditteridge asked, 'About what time did you go out this morning?'

'I think it was about ten o'clock,' she answered.

'So you got back about twelve. And the murder had probably happened by then. The doctor's rough guess is that the girl's been dead between seven and eight hours. What did you do when you got home? Did you go into her room?'

'I did, as a matter of fact. Just for a moment. I went in. Then – it was too silly . . .'

'Yes?' he said.

'I just went in to tidy up, you see,' she said. 'Sandra was awfully messy. I don't know if she ever made her bed when she was at home, or hung up any of her clothes. Anyway, I went in, and then for some stupid reason I panicked and bolted and slammed the door behind me and rushed downstairs. It was something to do with the shooting yesterday. I sort of felt that if I looked in the mirror I'd see that figure again with the gun pointing at me. So I didn't look in the wardrobe till I came home from the office in the afternoon. I wasn't feeling so nervy any more and I went into the room and started tidying up and – and I found her.'

'So you were out all the afternoon.'

'Yes, just as usual. And Lady Furnas came into the office and told us about having had her jewellery stolen. Edward darling, I haven't told you about that, have I? Althea came home from the Caribbean yesterday and found every scrap of her jewellery taken out of her safe. Every scrap, she said.' Martha looked at Mr Ditteridge. 'I suppose all these things are connected, aren't they? I mean, that theft, and Laurie Hassall coming down here, and his murder and Sandra's murder and now the way Derek's run out.'

'And the National Guild for the Welfare of Unmarried Mothers,' Mr Syme added with a quizzical grin. 'Do we write off the way they seem to keep cropping up as coincidence? The Chairman has her jewels stolen. Two unmarried mothers have kept getting under our feet from the beginning. The office is opposite the hotel where Hassall was murdered. Mrs Crayle, who works there, has been shot at and has found a dead body in one of her spare bedrooms. To me that seems three coincidences too many.'

'Can you explain them, then?' Mr Ditteridge asked rather absently, as if he had already been over all this in his own mind.

Mr Syme gave a grave shake of his head, but there was an unrevealing blandness on his face which Martha, who knew that at times he could be very secretive, thought was an indication that he was keeping a number of things to himself.

'There's one thing it might interest you to know,' Mr Ditteridge went on. 'Coombes has a perfect alibi for the time of Hassall's murder. And he has one for the time of Sandra Aspinall's as well. At the time when she was probably being strangled with the belt from her dress, he was in the police station, making a statement. There's no question about it. At the time when the girl was killed, he was telling Detective-Inspector Harrowby all about his whereabouts on Thursday afternoon, the time of Hassall's murder. Coombes's story's quite simple, and we've checked it. His mates at the printing firm where he works guaranteed that he was there all the afternoon as usual. So even if he came down to Helsington that evening, which he denies, he couldn't have got here much before seven. And doesn't Mr

Syme give him an alibi for the time of the shooting at you,
Mrs Crayle?'

She frowned reluctantly, reluctant to give up her belief
that Derek Coombes was responsible for both murders and
for the shooting at herself.

'Why did he want to make a statement to you?' she
asked. 'Isn't that suspicious?'

'Not really,' Mr Ditteridge said. 'We picked him up this
morning and asked him a lot of questions. At first it looked
as if he meant to be stubborn and tell us nothing, then all of
a sudden he decided to talk and tell us everything.'

'Or what he wanted you to think was everything.'

'Of course.'

'How did you know where to find him?'

'We had a man following him from the time he and the
girl left this house yesterday evening to go out and have
supper together. After Coombes brought her back he went
and got himself a room in one of the boarding houses in
Gadstow Place.' Gadstow Place was one of the few remaining terraces of Georgian houses left in Helsington and once
had had a modest sort of grandeur, though now it contained
only cheap boarding houses, some sleazy shops and offices
and one of the town's better-known brothels. 'He was still
in bed when we went for him about ten o'clock.'

'Then you let him go,' Martha said.

'We'd no reason for holding him.'

'No.'

She looked towards the door. She could hear a shuffling
of footsteps on the stairs and a murmuring of voices. Something made bumping sounds against the banisters. Mr Ditteridge got up and went out, closing the door behind him.
Martha heard the front door open and going to the window, she saw two men carry a covered stretcher to the
ambulance at the gate.

As it drove off Mr Ditteridge returned to the sitting-room and asked who would be staying in the house that night.

'I shall be here,' Mr Syme replied, 'and Mrs Crayle. I hope no one else. Though whether Lady Furnas or Miss Mason will send us some more unmarried mothers to house before the evening's out, I should not like to predict.'

'What nonsense, you know they won't,' Martha said. 'But I expect Amanda will be back. She's left her things here.'

'But you won't be here by yourself, Mrs Crayle?' Mr Ditteridge asked.

'No, no,' Mr Syme said. 'I shall see to that.'

'Good. Then good night and don't worry too much. I'll get in touch with you in the morning if there's anything of interest to report.'

'I only hope we don't have to get in touch with you before then,' Mr Syme said as he followed the detective to the door.

As it closed behind him it seemed to Martha that a silence and emptiness that was almost solid immediately settled on the house. She felt it as a kind of pressure on her temples, which throbbed abnormally in a way that might have frightened her if she had not known that it was simply the sympton of an intense excitement which she happened not to want to expose to anyone else. The sensation was one that she had experienced at other crises in her life, always at times when she felt determined to keep her feelings to herself. She took her head in her hands, feeling the beating of her pulses, and taking care not to look upward and meet Mr Syme's curious gaze, stared down at the flaring jets of the gas fire till their glow began to hurt her eyes and she started to see dark spots dancing before them.

'You're still sure he did it, in spite of all those alibis,' Mr Syme said. 'Are you going to tell me why?'

'What's the good?' she asked. 'You aren't going to believe me.'

'Well, those alibis are foolproof.'

'Isn't a thing that's foolproof only proof against fools?'

'I thought it meant something a bit different,' he said. 'I thought it meant something that even a fool couldn't get wrong.'

She shook her head and shut her eyes against the obsessive gleam of the fire.

'He did it,' she said, 'and I can explain nearly all of it to you, and someone as clever as you ought to be able to work out the rest. But we ought to be thinking of supper. There's cold chicken and some salad and I might open a tin of soup. I think I'd like something hot. The evening's so horribly cold. Or isn't it the evening? Is it just me? I can't stop shivering.'

'The evening's certainly turned colder,' Mr Syme said. 'It's been a long autumn, but you can't keep winter at bay for ever. But you're probably feeling the effects of shock as well. However, I find the thought of hot soup very acceptable, even if it only comes out of a tin. But there's no hurry. Tell me how you think you can break those three alibis?'

'That's the bit I was going to leave to you,' she said.

'Ah, I see.'

'Darling, you're so clever. Look at the way you found out how Sandra had been fooling us about Mr Gorton.'

'Poor Sandra. I wonder if my discovery had anything to do with her death.'

'Why should it?'

'I don't know. Just a thought. I never took to the child, but I should be sorry to have precipitated her murder. Particularly as she was pregnant. Isn't that the turn of the screw? That you can call it, in a sense, a double murder?'

Martha opened her eyes and looked at him thoughtfully. 'You keep surprising me,' she said. 'That thought's been giving me the creeps, but I'd never have expected it to get under your skin.'

'You have some very strange thoughts about me,' Mr

Syme replied. 'I am not inhuman. But now, about Coombes . . .'

Martha leant back in her chair, dropping her hands together in her lap.

'It's his motives that are so obvious, aren't they?' she said. 'Take Hassall. Hassall was a thief. When he got information that the right sort of house would be empty, he came along in daylight and burgled it. I don't know how he got the information. I suppose he picked a promising sort of district, then hung around the pubs and got talking to the servants and so on, till he found out what he wanted. But he'd have needed help, a look-out when he was on the job, someone to vanish away with the loot while Hassall himself went to some respectable hotel where he might stay for a day or two, behaving perfectly normally, with not a scrap of evidence to be found on him if the police somehow got suspicious of him.'

'Yes, well, so far I think I agree with you,' Mr Syme said.

'Well, the accomplice, of course, was Sandra. And I think it was Sandra being pregnant that gave her or Hassall the idea of using the Unmarried Mothers' as a look-out. They booked a room for Hassall in the Compton just across the street, and I'm sure you'll find they asked for a room that faced out over it, so that he could signal to Sandra, who'd have got into the office by then, that he'd got in from doing the job at the Furnases. I expect he switched a light on or off, or twitched a curtain, or something, and Sandra was supposed to go across, get the stuff from him and vanish from the scene as fast as she could. But instead, she signalled Derek, who probably had another room at the Compton, that Hassall was in his room, and Derek went there and was let in because Hassall was expecting Sandra, shot him, grabbed the Furnas stuff and did a bolt back to London. Sandra, of course, stayed put, so that Olive and I could give her an alibi for the whole afternoon.'

'But Coombes's alibi –'

'Let's leave those alibis for later. Though, as a matter of fact, I've got one or two ideas about them.'

'Well then, what turned the girl and Coombes against Hassall? What was their motive?'

'Perhaps she'd been Hassall's girl-friend till Derek came on the scene. Perhaps the child was Hassall's and that's why Derek wouldn't marry her unless she got rid of it. Or perhaps she'd got dissatisfied with the cut Hassall was giving her. Or perhaps the two of them just thought they'd make a better team without him.'

'But Coombes came here and tried to shoot the girl and later did kill her – isn't that your theory?'

She nodded. 'But first, the evening after Hassall's murder, she telephoned Derek in London to tell him there'd been an unfortunate mix-up and Amanda Hassall was staying here. They'd framed Amanda, of course – arranged for her to be in the Compton at the very time of the murder. But the ironic thing was, they didn't know she was pregnant too, and quite likely to come to us, seeing we were there, bang opposite the Compton. But once they found she was staying here they thought the sooner she was arrested the better, so when Derek had had the call from Sandra, he rang the police here and tipped them off where to find Amanda. And it was the day after that that he tried to shoot Sandra.'

'Why?'

'To have all the loot to himself. Or to get rid of a woman he'd got tired of perhaps.'

'But those alibis. I won't be put off any longer, my dear Martha. What do you really believe about those alibis?'

'Well, I suppose I think the first one, for Hassall's murder, was simply something he got fixed up with his friends,' Martha said. 'They probably knew quite well the sort of thing he was up to and were quite willing to cover up for him.'

'That's not impossible. But the second one, when I myself

saw him walking ahead of me at the very time that someone was shooting at you – what about that?'

She looked at him with a faint smile.

'Darling, your eyesight isn't absolutely perfect, is it?' she said. 'I know it's wonderful for your age, but still, suppose you saw someone get off the bus and walk along the Avenue some distance ahead of you – someone not unlike Derek, that's to say, a very ordinary-looking boy in the sort of clothes they all wear nowadays, and suppose that boy got into one of the parked cars near our gate and just sat there, lighting a cigarette or something, till you'd passed, could you swear, could you absolutely swear that it really was Derek you'd been watching and that you were sure he'd come in here?'

'And you mean the real Coombes got here some minutes earlier?'

'Yes.'

A tinge of pink appeared on Mr Syme's plump cheeks.

'I'm sure – I'm virtually sure – I'm all but certain . . . Oh well, I suppose I just possibly could have been mistaken, though I don't think I was. But what about this morning, when Coombes was actually in the police station when Sandra was being killed? You can't explain that away.'

'Not unless the doctor decides she was killed a good deal later than he thinks at present. I don't believe they can really be so awfully definite about that kind of thing. If there's any possibility she was killed in the afternoon, Derek could have done it.'

'Having got into the house, I suppose, by that broken window, always supposing you remembered to lock up when you went out after lunch. Well, I admit there's more to your theory than I thought there was going to be when you started, but there's just one thing I definitely don't like about it.'

Martha had got to her feet and was yawning. 'I really must get the supper,' she said, 'or I'll be too tired to stir.'

'Just a moment,' he said. 'Let me tell you what I don't like about your theory. I can't see why they should have got involved with the Unmarried Mothers', using that dangerous bogus reference and all. Suppose Miss Mason had checked it right away, they'd have been in trouble at once. And there was no need for that complicated signalling from the window of the office to Coombes. He only had to wait in the lounge of the hotel, as Mrs Hassall did, and follow Hassall up to his room when he came in.'

'Perhaps Amanda had seen him before and might have recognized him.'

Martha opened the door and crossed the hall to the kitchen.

In the doorway she stood still. She clapped a hand to her mouth. She wanted to scream, but something at the back of her mind said to her sternly, 'You've got to get on top of this. You're getting into the habit of screaming too easily. What's this, after all, compared with finding a body? What's an open window?'

For the broken window over the sink was wide open. A bitter wind was blowing in through it, ruffling the primrose curtains, and a square of starless sky showed dully black beyond the opening.

On the floor, leading from the sink to the door, were several large black footprints.

CHAPTER XII

MR SYME, who had followed Martha, put a hand on her shoulder and squeezed it as if he were afraid that that smothered scream might still come bursting out of her. They both stood very still, listening.

After a moment Martha whispered, 'He may be in the house still.'

Mr Syme frowned quickly to silence her. Martha could hear nothing but the traffic in the road, but all of a sudden Mr Syme gave a slight smile and moved soundlessly to the bottom of the stairs. He climbed them quickly. It astonished her how lightly the big, heavy man could move. Also, feeling very frightened herself, she was amazed at his lack of hesitation in going up to face whatever danger it was that had come in by that open window.

For it must have been something sinister. Anything innocent would have come to the front door and rung the bell in the normal way. Yet Mr Syme, portly, elderly, unarmed, was going upstairs to rout out this thing, this person, this evil. Then she remembered that war record of his, which was said to be so distinguished. She had always been hazy about just what decorations he had received, but as she stood rooted at the bottom of the stairs, she was convinced that he had deserved every one of them.

Then she heard him remark in his normal voice, 'I thought it might be you.'

It brought Martha to herself and sent her rushing up the stairs after him.

He was in the doorway of the room that had been Amanda's. Inside it, arrested in the middle of stuffing a pullover into Amanda's small overnight bag, was Don Turner. His red hair hung untidily about his ears. The scowl on his face was angrier than usual. He looked pale, but in a state of intense excitement which made Martha feel that there was no guessing what he might be capable of doing next.

'You stay out of this,' he said to Mr Syme. 'This has nothing to do with you.'

'Just so long as you don't mean to shoot up any more of Mrs Crayle's property,' Mr Syme said, standing solid and and composed in the doorway. 'Mirrors are not inexpensive.'

'I had nothing to do with shooting at Mrs Crayle,' the young man muttered.

'Did I say you had?'

'Didn't you?'

'No, I believe you shot at her mirror and up at her cornice, but that you had no intention of harming Mrs Crayle. Physically, that is. You seem to have been indifferent to the emotional shock you gave her.'

'You don't make sense.'

Martha broke in, 'Where's Amanda? What have you done with her?'

'She's in the garden,' Don Turner replied. 'She's waiting for me. And the sooner I can get her stuff together, the sooner I'll get out of your way.'

'In the *garden*?' Martha exclaimed. 'In *this* weather! She'll be frozen to death. Go and bring her inside immediately.'

Don hesitated. 'I'm not sure that she'll come. Seeing all the police, it was she who said she'd stay outside.'

'The police have all gone now,' Martha said.

'Yes, and at least you're alive – I'm glad of that.' He gave her his brief and wonderfully winning smile. 'You see, when we saw that stretcher come out, we didn't know what to think. It could have been you, or Mr Syme, or anybody.'

'It was Sandra.'

'*Sandra*? That girl who was here the other evening? Poor kid. What happened? Was she shot?'

'She was strangled.'

He drew his breath in sharply. There was a look of startled disbelief on his face.

But was that look genuine?

Martha found herself thinking how she was changing. The comfortable habit of believing that people meant what they said and that what she saw in their eyes truthfully expressed their feelings seemed to have slipped away from her.

She felt confused by her loss. She did not know how to think about anything. Her gaze dwelt on the big, strong hands that hung loosely at the young man's sides, hands which she could easily see tightening a cord about a slender young neck. A feeling of nausea began to mount in her throat.

'I'm going to fetch Amanda in,' she said, and turned and went downstairs.

Opening the front door and going out on to the doorstep, she called, 'Amanda! Come in!'

There was no answer. She called again.

A form detached itself from the bushes near the kitchen window.

'You found him, did you?' Amanda said. 'I told him you would.'

Martha took her by the hand, drew her into the house and closed the door. Amanda was wearing gloves, but even they felt ice-cold. The girl's face was blue and she was shivering all over.

'Whatever made you do a thing like this?' Martha asked, hurrying Amanda to the fireside in the sitting-room. 'Couldn't you see the police had gone?'

'Yes, I suppose it was stupid.' The girl's teeth were chattering. 'We were going to come to your door and ask for my things, because I'd decided to move in with Don at his motel and not bother you any more, then when I saw all the police cars in the street and someone carried out on a

stretcher, I felt, I simply insisted, I couldn't face any more
police just yet. I thought if I showed up they'd take me
back to the police station and there'd be more questioning.
And I wasn't feeling well and I just wanted to go somewhere warm and lie down. So we ducked into the bushes
and waited, and presently everyone went away and the
door shut. And that's when Don said he was going to nip
in by the kitchen window and get my things without troubling you at all, because, you see, we were afraid if you saw
us you'd just call the police again and hand us over for
suspicious behaviour or something.'

She had taken her gloves off and was holding out her
hands to the fire. Martha noticed that she was wearing a
wedding-ring, which she had not done before.

'Are you going to call the police?' Amanda asked. 'Even
if we haven't killed anybody, I suppose what Don did is
breaking and entering.'

Don, followed by Mr Syme, had just come into the room.
Don was carrying Amanda's bag.

'I'm not sure of the technicalities,' Mr Syme said, 'but I
don't believe Mr Turner's offence was actually breaking
and entering. The fact is, the window by which he entered
was already broken. And he certainly wasn't stealing anything that didn't belong to him. He was merely collecting
some possessions of his future wife's, hoping not to disturb
either of us after our very distressing and tiring day. Isn't
that how it was?'

Martha looked at Mr Syme in astonishment. His geniality was almost overpowering. For him, at least. She had
been expecting him to treat Don and Amanda to a dose of
stern reproach, at best to show his low opinion of the idiocy
of their behaviour and turn them out, at worst to do exactly
what they had feared and call the police. And here he was,
like a kindly old uncle, explaining the craziness of their
actions away.

It filled Martha with uneasiness. The distrustfulness that

had invaded her spirit that evening made her scent utter
falsity in Mr Syme. It also gave her that feeling that she had
tried to describe to Olive, of having earwigs crawling on her
skin. Also, as she very seldom had before, she felt a little
afraid of him.

'Oh yes, that's exactly how it was,' Amanda said.

'Good, good.' He actually rubbed his hands together.
'Very considerate of you really. And may I say how glad I
am to hear you're getting married. So very much the best
solution for you all. I'm sure your parents will be delighted.'

Mr Syme had overdone it, for Don gave him a faintly
amazed glance. Tapping Amanda on the shoulder, he held
out a hand to her.

'Come along,' he said. 'These people must have had
enough of us. They want a little peace and quiet, I shouldn't
wonder. And so do we. Thank you, Mrs Crayle, for being so
nice about things. Be seeing you at the inquest, shan't we?
We'll try not to get under your feet any more till then.
Good night.'

They all said good night and Mr Syme let Don and
Amanda out into the darkness.

Shutting the door behind them, he immediately fastened
the chain, something which he was not in the habit of
doing. Martha heard it jangle as he slipped it into the slot.
Returning to Martha, he startled her by giving her a short,
fierce hug, which almost took the breath out of her, then he
strode to the kitchen, saying, 'A drink – now I *really* need
a drink.'

Martha followed him. The window over the sink still
yawned. He slammed it shut.

'I'll nail some wood across that presently,' he said, 'but
now a drink.'

Martha did not quite believe what she saw, but she
thought that his hands were shaking. All the geniality had
gone from his voice and there was an unfamiliar wildness in
his eyes which were usually so blandly cool.

'The truth is, Martha my dear,' he went on jerkily, 'I am a coward. Fear upsets me terribly. I feel dreadful.'

She thought of how unhesitatingly he had climbed the stairs, not knowing what he would find at the top of them.

'But darling, you're a hero,' she said. 'Certified as such. Think of all those medals you've got.'

'I was young in those days,' he said. 'I believed in my own indestructibility. Now I'm old, slow on my feet and very attached to the remnant of life left to me. And I was unarmed just now. So I didn't like facing a powerful young thug who was almost certainly carrying a gun. Or if it was the girl outside who had the gun, that man could still have knocked me out with one blow and then dealt with you. I tell you I was a jelly of fear and I couldn't wait to get them out of the house.'

'Edward!' Martha said, looking at him with concern. 'Are you out of your senses? We agreed, didn't we, Derek's the murderer? Don and Amanda are absolutely harmless.'

'Derek was your idea,' he answered. 'I told you I'd reservations. And now, almost by accident, the private belief that I've held almost from the first has been confirmed. That's why, of course, I put on that revolting act of *bonhomie* just now. I hoped it might cover up the fact that I'd tumbled to the truth. I felt all the time my dreadful amiability wouldn't deceive a child and I was expecting to see a gun pointing at one or other of us at any moment, but I suppose the two of them were as anxious to get away as I was to get rid of them.' He grasped the whisky bottle and two glasses. 'Now let's go through to the other room – it's warmer in there – and I'll explain to you how things really happened.'

Martha stood still, frowning. 'Do you ever wonder if we drink too much?' she asked.

'We probably do, but this isn't the time to raise the question. Come along.'

In the sitting-room they sat down where they had sat

earlier, Mr Syme on a chair close to the gas fire, Martha on the hearthrug. She watched him broodingly as he poured out the drinks.

'I'm not going to agree with you, of course,' she said. 'Why should Don try to kill me?'

'He didn't try to kill you,' Mr Syme replied. 'Didn't I say so upstairs? He was very careful not to kill you.'

'But I thought you said . . . I thought you meant . . .' She shook her head, not sure what she thought that he had said or meant. 'Anyway, what's this about some private belief of yours being confirmed?'

'Don Turner came in by the kitchen window just now, didn't he?'

'Yes.'

'We know that for certain.'

'Yes.'

'We aren't guessing.'

'No.'

'He knew it was quite easy to get into the house that way. I know several other people knew about that window too, but who was as likely to know how easy it was to get in by it as the person who'd already used it? And the big muddy footmarks on the kitchen floor look to me exactly the same as the ones that were there yesterday when you were shot at.'

'You said I wasn't shot at.'

'Well, yes, that's correct. You were not the target. The shooting was done for only one purpose, to get those bullets into the hands of the police. They were bullets from the gun that killed Hassall. The fact that a mysterious figure was shooting at you with that gun when Amanda Hassall was in the hands of the police was meant to suggest that she had never had the gun and couldn't possibly have shot Hassall. When, of course, she could have, and did.'

'Just a minute. You remember how I screamed after that shooting. Didn't we decide it was because the man had really come to shoot Sandra, but had realized his mistake. And I'll tell you one thing, in case you didn't notice. When Sandra heard someone had been shooting at her, she was extremely angry, but she wasn't in the least surprised.'

'It isn't always possible to interpret facial expressions correctly. Anger, surprise, even fear, they can all look very like one another. But now tell me something. That figure you had a glimpse of on the landing, *could* it have been Turner, or is that simply impossible? Because if it's really impossible, my theory of course won't stand up.'

'Oh, it's possible, if he was crouching a bit,' Martha answered.

'Very well, I shall stick to my contention that it *was* Turner. That he'd broken the window earlier in the afternoon, while the house was empty. That he'd hidden in it until you got home. That he then followed you as soon as he could and let off those two shots, where you couldn't possibly fail to see where they'd gone, so that you'd be certain to report them to the police, but of course being careful not to hit you. And after that, he calculated, there was a good chance that Amanda Hassall would be set free, as she was.'

'But how did he get the gun?'

Mr Syme had drunk off his whisky faster than usual and was helping himself to some more. He reached out the bottle to top up Martha's glass but she shook her head. She had barely touched hers. Drink muddled her mind in a way that could often be very pleasant, but just now she wanted to keep it as clear as possible.

'From her suitcase, of course, when we thought he was running out on her,' Mr Syme said. 'But let's go back to the beginning. Let's start several years ago with the Hassalls' marriage. Amanda married Hassall, we were given to understand, without knowing much about him, believing him to be working in a firm of engineers. But trouble started almost at once. She discovered that he was really a thief and that wasn't the kind of thing to which a girl like her could comfortably adjust herself. But she didn't leave him or confide in her parents, partly out of pride, partly because her mother was besotted with his charm and would never have believed her, and partly because she clung to an idea that she might reform him. He played up to this by agreeing to take the job in Nairobi, but of course he intended to use it as a way of ditching her and slipping out of her life. Living with a naturally honest girl had undoubtedly been too much of a strain for him. What she would have done if that plane hadn't crashed and he hadn't been reported killed we don't know, but one thing I'm sure of. She would never have gone to the police to have him hunted down.'

'D'you know what I think she'd have done?' Martha said. 'I think she'd have gone off to Nairobi, pretending she was following him, and got a job there and never come back.'

Mr Syme nodded. 'Very possibly. However, that plane crash was very fortunate for everyone, except for the unlucky people who happened to have been on board. Hassall himself was free, Amanda had got rid of her undesirable husband with her face saved, and the Gravelys were able to mourn their son-in-law as dotingly as they pleased without ever having to be told the truth about him. But then Don Turner appeared on the scene.'

'I don't really understand why she didn't marry him right away,' Martha said. 'At that time she believed her husband was dead.'

'Why won't you marry me?' Mr Syme said. 'You've a prejudice against marriage due to past experience, isn't that all?'

'We won't go into that now. Why shouldn't she have married him?'

'Precisely for that reason, a prejudice based on limited and unfortunate experience. And I should think it gave her a certain satisfaction to distress her parents, whose blindness concerning Hassall she doesn't seem able to forgive.

And then, of course, soon after she became pregnant and was probably seriously considering marrying Turner, she actually saw Hassall in the Piccadilly Underground. So marriage was out of the question for the moment. Then, when she tried to tell Turner and her parents that she had seen Hassall, they all leapt to the conclusion it was a delusion, the result of the unstable state of mind that I believe affects some women during pregnancy.'

'Then she had that telephone call telling her where she could find Laurie. But how did they know where to find her?'

'I suspect that when Hassall seemed to run away from her at Piccadilly, he really turned back and followed her and found out where she was living with Turner.'

'But why should anyone want her to meet Laurie if it wasn't to frame her for a murder that someone else meant to commit?'

'I'm sure it *was* to frame her.'

'And then she shot Laurie before this other person could get to him?'

'Exactly.'

'So Derek *meant* to murder Laurie, and then Amanda did it for him. Because there are the jewels, you see. You mustn't forget them. Amanda might have done a murder, but she'd never have helped herself to a lot of stolen jewels. Yet Laurie must have had them on him when he was killed, and they're missing now. So someone took them, and I believe it was Derek.'

'A good point,' Mr Syme said. 'Yes, I'm sure you're right.'

'But in that case, why shouldn't Derek have done the murder too?'

'Because Amanda had the gun when she came here. How else did it get into Turner's possession? She shot Hassall, then put the gun into that bag she carries around, which was up in her room when we were all down here, discussing what had happened. And she accused Turner of believing that she'd done the murder and he suddenly got up and walked out. He did believe she'd done the murder. But he'd just made up his mind to find out for certain if she had or not, so that he could think out how to help her. He went upstairs to see if she'd got the gun, found it and got it out of the house before there was any risk of the police arriving. Then, next day, he used it to do his shooting act here. And after that I imagine it went into the river, or some such place where it'll never be found.'

'But why kill Sandra?'

'I imagine she knew rather more than was healthy for her. She'd been at your office window, remember, and Coombes probably told her how things had happened at the Compton. So when she found Amanda and Turner in the kitchen here this morning she must have let them see how much she knew, or may even have tried to blackmail them. Then, when they'd dealt with her, they washed up their own breakfast things and put them tidily away, and put out those two cups you found, with the coffee and the milk bottle, to make you believe she'd had a visitor. Then they cleared out. But unfortunately, in the excitement of committing a murder, they forgot to take Amanda's bag away with them, so they had to come back for it this evening.'

Martha gave a deep sigh. A leaden depression had crept up on her while Mr Syme was talking which the whisky seemed only to be making worse. She had liked Amanda. Imagining her as a murderess produced an actual physical sensation of acute discomfort. Most of her joints had begun to ache. But perhaps that was because she was getting a little old for sitting on the floor, or even was developing Olive's flu.

Standing up, she said, 'I'll get the supper now. And you're going to telephone the police, I suppose, to tell them all this. They'll have to be told about Don breaking in here.'

She went out to the kitchen, took the cold chicken out of the refrigerator and began listlessly mixing a salad.

While she was doing it, she heard Mr Syme speaking on the telephone, she supposed to Mr Ditteridge, but she did not pay much attention. She was even tireder than she had realized. Yet that night she slept very little. This was unusual for her. Generally in times of crisis she plunged into deep, dreamless sleep from which she awoke in the morning feeling doped and stupid, but which at least had given her several hours of escape from her troubles. Tonight, however, she was possessed by a fiendish restlessness. In whatever position she lay, her joints went on aching, and she could not stop herself listening for the slightest sound of movement in the house. She did not know what she was listening for. Mr Syme had nailed some wooden slats across the broken window and she was not really afraid of another intruder coming in by that way, yet she felt fear of something, fear that pursued her into the few snatches of sleep that she achieved and gave her nightmares. It was daylight before she fell into a fairly calm sleep, from which she felt she was wakened almost immediately by the ringing of the telephone by her bed.

She reached out for the telephone and drowsily mumbled her number into it. Her head was aching and she had a sore throat. It was certainly Olive's flu.

'Martha?' It was Althea's voice. 'I've just been seeing some more of the police about our burglary, and they told me about your finding the body of that girl Sandra in your house, and I've been thinking how awful for you and wondering how you were.'

'Well, that sort of thing takes it out of you,' Martha replied. 'As a matter of fact, it was quite hideous, but I'm quite all right, so to speak.'

'Look then, if you're feeling up to it, I think you and Olive and I ought to have a talk. Don't you think that would be a good idea?'

'If you want it, though I don't know what about. Mr Syme has solved the crime.'

'He has? Isn't that just like him? Such an intelligent man. I've always admired him. But it's the Press and publicity and that sort of thing that I think we ought to talk about. There hasn't been much publicity so far, but I'm awfully afraid it's coming. The Unmarried Mothers angle is going to strike someone suddenly and we're going to find ourselves surrounded. And that won't be at all good for the organization – above all not good for the girls in the hostel now. You know what they're like. They'll get morbidly excited about it all and pour out all kinds of unlikely stories to any reporter who goes near them. And the Committee won't approve and will probably blame us for handling things badly. So I thought a quiet talk this morning might be useful, to make sure we all take the same line. I thought the office would be the best place for it. We aren't likely to be disturbed there on a Sunday morning. I've already spoken to Olive about it and she's coming.'

'I see. Yes, all right.' Martha swung her feet to the floor. 'What time d'you want me to get there?'

'Can you manage in about an hour?'

'Yes.'

If she took two aspirins now, Martha thought, they would have had time to work in an hour and she would arrive at the meeting tolerably clear-headed. Some strong black coffee too might help. Putting on her dressing-gown, she went downstairs to make the coffee.

She was the last of the three women to arrive at the office. Althea Furnas, perched on the edge of Martha's desk, was wearing her tatty mink and an expression of abstracted worry as she listened to Olive who was standing at the window, staring at the Compton Hotel as if the place had an obsessive interest for her. She had on her black knitted hood and her sheepskin jacket over her dark green twin-set and tweed skirt. She looked better than when Martha had seen her last and her voice had lost most of its hoarseness.

She was saying, 'We'll survive, you know. Some publicity may even do us good. People who've never heard of us may send us donations. It isn't as if they can tie us in with the crimes. A pack of bloody thieves falling out and making a balls up of polishing one another off in Helsington hasn't anything to do with us. I know, by an accident, Martha's had to bear the brunt – Martha, Althea's just told me about that girl Sandra – I can't tell you how sorry I am. It must have been hell for you, and I blame myself for not taking up her references – '

From behind Martha the voice of Superintendent Ditteridge interrupted, 'About that reference, Miss Mason, don't you usually require a medical report as well as a character reference?'

He had come quietly into the room and was standing just inside the doorway with a uniformed sergeant behind him.

Olive turned to him with a startled look.

'Of course,' she said. 'We should certainly have looked into that side of things as soon as possible. But I wasn't well. I was muddled. I wasn't as careful as I should have been.'

'Would it have surprised you to know that Sandra Aspinall was no more pregnant than I am?' he asked.

Althea gave a little whistle. Olive and Martha looked at him in silence.

'It's partly to discuss that interesting point that I asked you to get your friends here this morning, Lady Furnas,' Mr Ditteridge went on. 'It's an odd fact, you see, that right from the start there's been a curious connection between the National Guild for the Welfare of Unmarried Mothers and the murder of Lawrence Hassall. A connection it's been easy to write off as coincidence. It happened that a murder was committed in a hotel across the street from your office. It happened that two unmarried mothers were somehow involved. But why should that have anything to do with you? Why indeed? That seems the obvious way to think. But suppose you turn it the other way round. Suppose you ask yourself if Hassall could have been murdered in that hotel *because it was across the street from this office*. Suppose a room was booked for him in that hotel and facing on to this street just so that someone standing at the window here could look into his window and see when he'd got there after burgling the Furnas home?'

'You mean Sandra . . .' Martha began uncertainly. Then she shook her head. 'How did she know Miss Mason would let her sit here all that afternoon? How did Sandra know Miss Mason wouldn't take up that reference from Mr Gorton straight away and ask for a medical report?'

'How indeed, unless she and Miss Mason had arranged the matter beforehand?' Mr Ditteridge said.

Martha looked quickly at Olive Mason. So did Althea Furnas. Olive said nothing, but her face had gone grey-white, like dough that has been handled too much.

'Miss Mason's part in all these events is very interesting,' Mr Ditteridge went on. 'There have been a good many burglaries in the district recently, and it happens that she, with all her varied connections in the town, is in a singularly good position to hand on information about what houses are likely to be empty at what times. She could be very useful to certain people she knew. Among them was Hassall, a skilled thief, only unfortunately not reliable. When he got drunk, he talked too much. He must have done something that frightened the rest of the gang, which decided them to get rid of him. And they set up the situation here so that Sandra could keep a watch on that window across there till Hassall got in and also give Miss Mason an alibi when she cut across the road and shot Hassall and made off with Lady Furnas's jewels. She sent you out, didn't she, Mrs Crayle, to get her prescription for her, knowing that would take you some time, immediately Sandra gave her a signal of some sort. I don't know what the signal was – '

'She said – Sandra said – "Wouldn't some tea do your cough good, Miss Mason?" ' Martha suddenly remembered. 'But why should it have been Miss Mason who did the shooting? Why not Sandra?'

'Because Sandra herself is dead now,' Mr Ditteridge answered. 'And for an ironically insufficient reason. She believed that Olive Mason, who'd already murdered once, had come to your house and tried to shoot her, nearly shooting you by mistake. Sandra believed Miss Mason must want to get rid of her as she'd already got rid of Hassall. The girl didn't realize the shots were fired by Don Turner, trying to set up a rather crude kind of alibi for Amanda Hassall, and that he wasn't shooting at anybody. So Sandra waited till she was alone in the house yesterday morning, then telephoned Miss Mason, who came over immediately. They had coffee together, or we must suppose so, though we didn't find Miss Mason's fingerprints on the jar. Then Sandra was so very stupid as to threaten Miss Mason with exposure. She thought she was protecting herself. In fact, she could not have made a worse mistake. Miss Mason is a very strong woman and she didn't wait for further trouble. She knocked Sandra unconscious, then strangled her with the belt of the dress she was wearing. Then she carried her upstairs and stowed her in the wardrobe where you found the body many hours later. I would add that Derek Mason, known as Derek Coombes, a brother of Miss Mason's, through whom she became involved in her criminal activities, was arrested yesterday evening when he reached London and has talked freely. He says we shall find Lady Furnas's jewellery in Miss Mason's flat. Olive Mason, it is my duty to inform you – '

But the remaining words of the official warning were drowned by peal after peal of laughter that suddenly started pouring out of Olive's throat. Her mouth was dragged down to one side of her face in what looked almost like a gleefully sardonic grimace.

'Martha, Martha!' she crowed. 'If you could see your-self! Remember me saying I wondered how you'd look if you found yourself face to face with someone really evil? Well, now I know! Oh, if you could see yourself!'

The laughter seemed to grow louder and louder till the room was filled with it.

CHAPTER XIII

'OF COURSE, she isn't all evil,' Martha said later in the day.

She was in bed with a temperature of a hundred and one. Mr Syme had insisted on calling in the doctor. He was an old friend of Martha's, who had delivered her babies and helped to look after Aunt Gabrielle. Besides that, he lived close by in Blaydon Avenue, so it had not been too difficult to prise him out of his Sunday afternoon game of bridge for a quarter of an hour to come and prescribe an anti-biotic. Mr Syme had set out with the prescription to the one chemist in Helsington who stayed open on a Sunday, had brought back the tablets and added his own remedy to them, a long glass of whisky, lemon and hot water.

Martha sipped the hot drink gratefully. Her throat felt as raw as if it had been sandpapered, her eyes and her nose were beginning to run and cold shivers kept running up and down her veins while her skin felt burning. Yet she had a light-headed compulsion to talk which she could not control.

'Think of the good she did for all those girls,' she said. 'Doesn't that count? I realize now all her good works must have bored her dreadfully, or she'd never have got involved in stealing, yet she was immensely efficient, you know. She helped far more people than you and I ever have in our lives. And they appreciated it. You should have seen all the Christmas cards she got every year, and the photographs of the babies the girls used to send her, and sometimes invitations to weddings. Oh, there was a lot of good in Olive, I'm certain of that.'

'All right, if it makes you happy to think so,' Mr Syme replied. He was sitting on a chair near Martha's bed, also sipping a hot whisky and lemon, perhaps for prophylactic purposes. 'Now what are we going to do about your supper? You know I'm not a competent cook. Shall I go to the Chinese and get a carry-out meal? King prawn chow mein or something like that.'

Martha shook her head. 'I haven't any appetite at all. You go and have a good dinner at your club and I'll get myself a boiled egg by and by. That's all I want.'

'No, you mustn't get up,' Mr Syme said. 'And I don't think you ought to be left alone. You aren't looking at all well. But it would only take me a few minutes to go round to the Chinese. I thought you liked their king prawn chow mein.'

'Oh, all right, if that's what you want,' she said. 'I was just thinking, d'you remember telling me how some nurse of yours said things always came in threes? Well, I think this flu is my third thing.'

'Just drink up your whisky then. It'll do you good.'

'It's very nice and soothing. But darling, I do want you to understand about Olive – '

'Don't worry about her. She's no affair of ours any longer.'

'Well, there's something that's puzzling me still. The gun. How did it get from hand to hand? Olive had it when she shot Laurie Hassall, but Don had it when he did the shooting here.'

'Don't you see, Sandra Aspinall had it when she came to the house,' Mr Syme replied. 'Olive Mason gave it to her to get rid of, and the girl, finding she was in the same house as Amanda Hassall, popped it into Mrs Hassall's suitcase. I seem to remember seeing it in the sitting-room when we were all fussing around after Mrs Hassall fainted.'

'That's right, I took the case upstairs myself later when we were trying to get Amanda to lie down.'

'Well, if the police had found it there, it would just about have clinched the case against Mrs Hassall, wouldn't it?'

'D'you know, I rather wish you wouldn't call her Mrs

Hassall,' Martha said. 'Why d'you find it so difficult to call people by their first names?'

'Because for my generation it's a sign of intimacy and I feel no sort of intimacy with the young woman. But I'll try to remember to call her Mrs Turner, if you prefer.'

'I think that might only confuse me. Go on.'

'You know the rest of it. Turner thought of the possibility of the gun being in the bag, because he really believed Mrs Hassall – Amanda – had killed her husband. Finding the gun, naturally, made him sure of it. His loyalty to her, in the circumstances, was extraordinary. I hope she appreciates it.'

'I'm sure she does. I expect they'll be very happy. About Olive – '

'Martha, my dear, must we really talk about that dreadful person? The sort of good qualities she had make me think of the kind of criminal who, I believe, sometimes donates large sums of money to charity while organizing large-scale robbery and murder. In my view it does not make up for greed, cruelty and treachery.'

'But we worked together, don't you understand?' Martha said. 'We got on all right. Anyway, how can we help being the sort of people we are? It's probably all a matter of chromosomes.'

'Perhaps it's also a matter of chromosomes with people like you,' Mr Syme said with his aloof smile. 'You can't reform them any more than you can a criminal. The chronically good and tolerant can be utterly incurable. Now about our supper, I shan't be gone long unless there's a queue.' He stood up. 'Anyway, you'll be giving up the Unmarried Mothers, won't you? They'll have to reorganize themselves completely. For one thing, they'll have to get a new secretary, and you may find you can't get on with her nearly as well as with the estimable Miss Mason.'

'Now you're being horrid. Go away and get our supper.'

'You see, I don't believe I could bear it if I were to find any more of those so-called unfortunate girls lurking furtively about the house. The next ones might come armed with knives or poison.'

'If you don't feel safe here, you can always move out, can't you?'

His face turned cold and haughty. 'Martha, that's a very cruel thing to say, very cruel,' he said. 'It doesn't sound like you.'

'No, and of course I don't mean it,' she said. 'I couldn't bear it if you went away. All the same, I've been thinking we don't need this great big house, do we? It's just a temptation to bring people home. So I think it would be sensible to split it in two and make the top half into a nice flat which I could sell for quite a lot of money, and in the lower one there'd still be room for you and me and a spare room for the boys, and we could get rid of poor Aunt Gabrielle's awful furniture and buy some nice things, and of course redecorate –'

'Splendid, splendid!' Mr Syme broke in enthusiastically. 'That's the best idea you've had for a very long time. And you'd be so busy, organizing it all, that you wouldn't have time to do some miserable voluntary job, would you? And one day soon, when you're feeling better, we might get around to that question of marriage again. I don't think you've ever given it the consideration it deserves.'

Martha looked thoughtful. Her touch of fever and the whisky were making the room swim slightly.

'Of course, the boys would be pleased if I married,' she said. 'They'd think of it as a sort of provision for my old age, which I think they sometimes worry about.'

'Now stop, stop!' Mr Syme shouted at her. 'I refuse to marry you because your sons think it would be a good idea. When you yourself think it's a good idea, please inform me. Till then, I shall not refer to the subject again.'

'It just seems to me we're very happy as we are.'

Mr Syme pursed his lips, as if he had some difficulty in keeping back the retort that came to them. Picking up the two empty glasses, he tramped away down the stairs. Martha heard the front door close after him and the squeak of the garden gate as he set off to the local Chinese restaurant.

She lay back, feeling distinctly ill, yet in some way not uncomfortable. In the silent house she soon grew drowsy. Her eyelids felt heavy and her aching limbs seemed to be floating instead of lying inert in the bed. Her thoughts, instead of being all too active, as they had been some minutes before, became blurred and unable to fasten themselves upon any particular point for more than a moment. Of course she had no intention of giving up her work for the Guild, but this was not the time to argue about it. It was so pleasant to be cherished.

Presently she slept a little, and did not waken until heavy footsteps returned up the stairs, accompanied by the clink of china and the unmistakable odour of king prawn chow mein.